Blind Beauty

....

Kalia Miller

Contents

Blind Beauty | 1

A /n: this is my first try at fantasy; hope i don't suck! :D

EDITED.

Chapter Uno

Arlette breathed in profoundly. As always, she was mesmerized by the scent the blooming flowers gave off around her. She danced around a little more. She always liked this place. It was quiet and peaceful. She could hear the little birds chirping softly around her, the wind blowing her fiery, red hair as she twirled around. Doing so, she could feel the tender, tingling sensation of the flowers beside her feet, making her smile. She could hear the children giggle in the distance, running and squealing around.

The meadow was her favorite place to be. It always gave her the remarkable feeling that she could be in touch with nature and with everything else. She threw her head back, letting the dying sun hit her face and kiss her skin. She could feel its heat, and it sure signaled it was quite hot today. Then, at last, she collapsed, her back touching the ground, and her front facing the sky.

"Arlette, supper's ready!" Shouted her grandma from the cottage.

A heavy sigh escaped Arlette's lips, as the opportunity of having free time disappeared in an instant, and then got back up, going through her dress pocket and grabbing her cane. She didn't need it though, she knew her way back, but just so that her grandma wouldn't freak out, she'd gladly use it. She'd gotten the cane from the 'outside' world, where humans lived, when she was younger. She remembered when no witch or healer could find her something that would be able to guide her. That is, until her uncle decided that he would go outside of the Lands, where medication was more advanced.

Living without a cane wasn't so difficult for Arlette. When she was younger, she could identify almost everything around her without any inconveniences. She could walk through her cottage without tripping, walk through the fields without getting lost... but her mother, as always, wanted the best for her and her sisters.

There was some controversy, of course; they weren't supposed to get anything from the outside world, but she desperately needed it, as her mother said, and there was no other option.

She walked towards her family cottage, enjoying the familiarity of it. She had lived here all her life, and she wouldn't want to change it for anything, this place was perfect. It was where her sisters and she grew up. It was where she got to know what a family was like. She could recall all the memories. The laughing, the crying, the hugging...

Arlette stifled a laugh; back then, her sisters were amazing, always worrying about her, always protecting her from rude, ignorant kids—how the other kids would pout and cry because her sisters had given them a good piece of them. Those were good times, good memories. But it changed– everything did. Because when men started laying eyes on her sisters once they were growing up, Arlette was slowly being pushed back.

At first, she couldn't understand what was happening, but when her sisters explained it to her, the whole thing became crystal clear.

Stepping into the cottage, and closing the door behind her, she was met by strong scents. She scrunched up her nose at the smell. Too much. What was her grandma cooking? She carefully made her way to the kitchen. The scents becoming slightly stronger the closer she got. Everyone was in the kitchen already; she could hear them—her sisters chatting animatedly, her mom talking to her dad about how he should go somewhere to cure his constant coughing, and her grandma going through the drawers doing Lord knows what.

"Oh, Arlette, finally, you're here. We were waiting for you," she heard her mom say tenderly as she took a seat in one of the chairs. Closing her cane, she put it back in her dress pocket.

She nodded wordlessly, following where she heard her mother's voice.

A couple of minutes later, everyone was eating and talking aimlessly, Arlette not paying much attention to any of the conversation that was going on. However, one of her sisters mentioned something that made her head slowly follow her dramatic voice.

"Did you hear? The King is worried that his son, the Prince, won't find his princess." That was Ember talking, her older sister. Ember had very long, pale blonde hair that went down her waist, and she was tall with green eyes. Very beautiful. At least, that's how her mom had described her.

Before her other sister could respond to that, Arlette's mom sighed, she could hear her putting her fork down, "I'm sure we all know why, Ember, there's no need to talk about it."

But Arlette didn't know, so despite her mom's warning to end the conversation, she turned her head to where she had heard Ember talking, and asked, "Why?"

"Arlette..." her father warned, coughing, obviously not wanting to talk about the King's son.

"Because my dear Arlette, the Prince is a beast," answered Ember dramatically, not listening to either of her parents.

"That's enough, Ember!" her grandma bellowed, slapping the table as she got up, exasperated.

How come Arlette didn't know about this when everyone else in the family clearly did? And it specifically looked like a delicate topic. She once again felt like she was the last one to know everything. Even if it was the smallest thing, she was always the last one to know about it, and it made her blood boil.

After that, everyone finished eating in a heavy, stupidly awkward silence. Arlette was still thinking about the Prince and how Ember had describe him as a beast. What did she mean? Did he act like a beast? Heartless and cruel? Or was he a beast—deformed and ugly? Or was he both? All those questions lurked around her mind, making her wonder.

Arlette's mom broke the silence, "We don't want you girls to talk about the King's son in this house, we all know is a delicate topic—"

"Mom, everyone in the village talks about him," Cade, her other sister, cut in, and Arlette could almost swear that she rolled her eyes. Cade, as her mom had described her, was also tall, though with brunette curls and blue eyes.

All three of them were different. Especially Arlette. Arlette had fiery, red hair that fell down her waist in heavy waves. She had brimming hazel eyes, and a delicate, heart shaped face. Her mom had told to her that she wasn't as tall as her sisters, but an average height. Her mom said that she was also very beautiful, but Arlette concluded not as much as her sisters.

"We're very aware of that, Cade. But the King warned all of us through letters, and we should follow his desires," her mom said calmly, pushing the chair, indicating that she had gotten up.

Arlette also excused herself to bed, and strangely, her mom decided to guide her, lacing her arm through hers.

"Mom, I know my way."

"I know you do, sweetie. I just want to talk to you."

Closing the door behind her, Arlette unlaced her arm from her mother's, making her way to her bed, taking her shoes off, and sitting comfortably. She liked the smell of her room. It smelled like flowers and peaches, something she had always loved.

She was warily angry with her mother—and with everyone in her family at that. And her mom knew that.

"Arlette, I'm sorry I didn't tell you sooner about the letter—" Her mom started to say, but Arlette interrupted her.

"Not that you had any plans to, mom. But tell me, why must I be the last one to know everything?" Arlette was furious, but she talked calmly to her mom, which was something that incredibly surprised her. She could hear her mom as she sat in the leather chair beside Arlette's bed, murmuring something to herself.

She sighed. "We just don't want any of you girls to be in danger," and before Arlette could ask why on earth would they be in danger, her mom continued, "I'm going to tell you a story Arlette, and I want you to listen good,"

Arlette silently nodded, now confused as ever. She could hear the seriousness is her mother's voice, and that terrified her. She knew that her father was a good friend of the King, but surely nothing had happened between them?

"All these years, there's been a rumor that someone related to the King was cursed by an evil, sadistic witch. I'm sure you've heard of it?" Arlette's mom paused, and Arlette nodded. "Well, as expected, it's his son—he's been cursed. Nobody really knows why, but as always, rumors speak for it." Her mom paused.

Arlette knew that there were a very low percentage of evil witches in the Fae Lands; they were usually good, calmly minding their own business. They often were against the evil, and helped anyone who needed them. But there also were very, very evil witches who use their great powers to their advantage, causing immense damage and such.

"What are the rumors?" Arlette asked, swallowing the lump in her throat. She hated these types of stories.

"A very long time ago, the handsome Prince fell in love with a young, beautiful lady. She was the woman of his life, he'd say. He was going to marry her. They seemed like the perfect couple. Fate was at their side.

The young lady was strange though..." she paused. "Turns out, one day, when the Prince was going up the stairs to his room, he found her kissing one of the guardians. He was torn and furious and decided to end their relationship. But the girl begged and begged him to forgive her, saying that Fate wanted them together; the Prince wasn't having that though."

"It was her turn to be furious then. The girl turned out to be a witch and in her despair, cursed him for his little mistake—making him cruel and heartless and lonely, distorting his face to the point where he looked like a beast."

Arlette gasped, but her mom continued, "The point is, Arlette, that he is very dangerous and your father, grandma nor I want you and your sisters to talk about him. It's true, he needs a princess after all these years of lone-liness, but he is doomed to be alone. His father doesn't understand that though. He's determined to look for a young lady who would accompany his son in the throne—"

"Mom, get to the point," Arlette urged, feeling like her mom was taking too long.

"He'll soon be sending guards to take every female and bring them to the palace, letting the Prince decide whom he would want to be his princess." She finally finished.

Arlette felt like she was choking on thin air, her eyes widened and her stomach clenched as her mom's words sank in deep in her head.

Her mom came to her side in one instant, taking Arlette's trembling hands in hers. Arlette could sense her mother's fear as it tingled in her hands, a gift she had—to feel through people's feelings and emotions. "Sweetie, that's why we're trying to hide you and your sisters from him, but it's really difficult when the King already knows that your father and I have three daughters."

comment and vote, k? it makes me happy.

Blind Beauty | 2

Credits to coptherobber for the amazing banner on the side!

EDITED.

Chapter Dos

Arlette stayed awake all night—thinking and thinking about what her mother said to her—how her and her father were protecting her and her sisters. Especially her though. They were much more worried about Arlette than Ember and Cade, they could take care of themselves, Arlette "couldn't", as her mother had put it. Arlette and her mother were arguing vividly about this the night before. She, in no means, wanted to feel so... helpless.

Her mother had said that she was under her parents protection, and that nothing will ever happen to her.

She had asked about her sisters, what would happen to them if one of them got chosen. Her mother just sighed and said that they'd go through it, they could take care of themselves; they were grown-ups, after all, and so Arlette shouldn't worry very much about her sisters or anyone else, but herself.

Arlette thought her mother was being somewhat selfish, if not bias. Worrying about her but not her sisters? She frowned at that.

Walking out of her room, she skimmed her hands down her long, heavy dress. Arlette was pulling on it slightly as it was a bit tight for her liking, but she figured that it'll do. Her mother had picked it out for her, and she wasn't about to have an argument about how tight her dress was with her mother. Her mother was...complex. A really incomprehensible creature.

Stepping into the kitchen like every morning, she was greeted by her mom and grandmother.

"Where's dad?" Arlette asked, curious, as she sat down. She couldn't feel his presence here, not even his manly scent.

"Oh, your mother sent him to a healer, dear. He has gotten worse." Her grandma answered, pulling a chair and sitting down. She sounded exhausted.

The fact that Arlette's dad had gotten worse was something that deeply worried her. He had never been this sick, not even when the early plague attacked the place he had been going through a couple of years ago. This wasn't a good sign. In fact, this was a really, really bad sign, and if the healer can't cure him, there were going to be some serious problems.

"He's a very experienced healer..." She heard her mother inquire through the mists of her whirling thoughts. Her mother wanted to convince herself, that was something Arlette was certain. Hopefully, his healing abilities were strong and powerful enough to cure him... But it didn't really matter if he was an experienced healer or not. When Fate said no, it didn't matter if it was a sting of a bee, it was a no, and that was what scared Arlette the most.

Ember had entered the kitchen, her presence heavy and uncomfortable. She greeted her mother then grandma, and at last, Arlette. She must've been upset about something—her stiff voice and movements automatically gave it off. She pulled out a chair, and slumped down.

"I couldn't sleep," Ember finally clarified, sighing. "There were ninnies flying all over my room...they wouldn't leave me alone,"

"Was your window open?" Her grandma asked. All three of them were sitting in the kitchen, finishing breakfast. The only one missing was Cade—she always woke up late.

Ember sighed. "Yes. I thought I'd closed it..."

Ninnies were incredibly annoying, little fairies. They were as small and fragile as petals, but their constant buzzing and silliness to "play" was beyond upsetting. They didn't really do anything other than come out at night and "play", which actually meant that they were looking for any living thing to bug on. Arlette couldn't blame Ember for that one. They were indeed stressing.

Cade came in at last, her presence graceful and happy as ever. Arlette frowned at her behavior. Something must have pinched her in her sleep, Arlette thought, greeting Cade as well. By the time Cade started to eat breakfast, Arlette had excused herself to go to her favorite place— the meadow.

"Wear your cloak, Arlette." her mother had instructed when she had gotten up.

Arlette frowned, turning to where she felt her mom's presence. "I'm not going outside the meadow, mom. Since when do I have to wear a cloak while outside of the village's streets?" she asked, slightly irritated. This was unusual of her mother.

"Since now, Arlette." she inquired sternly. "Now, put this on," she shoved Arlette's cloak into her hands.

Arlette groaned, giving up, and slowly, frustratingly, shrugged her big, dark cloak on with a huff. Once she'd put it on, she headed as fast as she could towards the front door, but her mom's voice stopped her.

"Cover your hair!"

She let out an irritated breath, taking the cloak's hood and smoothly placing it over her head.

"Satisfied?" Arlette asked, her voice covered with irritation.

"Yes, very. You can go now."

"Gods..." Arlette murmured as she opened the front door. Her mother could really be a handful sometimes.

As she stepped into the meadow, she instantly knew that there was a very little percentage she would enjoy herself with this cloak, so instead, she just collapsed between the chirping daisies, her front facing the sky.

They were supposed to wear cloaks when they were outside their house and into the village puzzling depths, not on her family's territory.

Only females were required to wear cloaks when they were outside of their cottages. It showed something about self-respect and dignity, something all females should have.

The sun kissed Arlette's face potently, soon making her have beads of sweat roll down her forehead.

She pushed herself up in a sitting position, taking her cloak's hood off so she could get some fresh air through her sweaty neck and hair. Maybe it was better to go inside the cottage, where the sun wasn't so much of a murderer.

The wind suddenly picked up, and blew Arlette's hair out of her face. She sighed happily, closing her eyes and breathing in the many different scents the wind brought. The damp grass, the smell of the smoke that came from people's cottages, indicating that they were cooking, the soothing scent of the flowers... those were the little things that made Arlette happy, and for a brief moment, it made her want to see what was around her—what it would be like to actually see colors - to actually see her family's faces...She shook her head, telling herself to never want nor wish any of those things; she knew she'd never get them.

And then, out of nowhere, the wind brought an utter, dreading smell, making Arlette desperately cover her nose and mouth with her hand. What was that stench? She got up, and suddenly the wind got stronger and she no longer could feel the heat of the sun, but hear ominous thundering and clashing in distance, rapidly getting closer.

Un-bearing fear crawled up Arlette's spine as she hurriedly walked back towards the cottage. She practically ran, not caring if she used her cane or not. And when she felt like she was right in front of the door, she threw the door open to sickly hear her mother shouting desperately.

"We're being attacked!"

Blind Beauty | 3

Forgot who made the banner but there it is!

EDITED.

Chapter Tres

"Ember, get the carriage!"

They ran as fast as they could out of the cottage, picking up just a few necessities and throwing them in the carriage. It felt as if there were big oak trees falling from the sky when the ground shook aggressively beneath them.

Arlette could hear the poor horse whinnying in fear as it was being tied to the carriage. She flinched at the thundering, ear-splitting sound that came from the sky when her mom was grabbing her hand violently and pushing her inside the vehicle. She could also smell the suffocating stench of smoke coming from the meadow, and she wished it wasn't what she was thinking.

And then it hit her. Her village was being destroyed.

She could hear the agonizing screaming of women and children, and the yelling of men to get carriages.

"No, no, no, no, no..." She whispered over and over again as she heard her father's voice yelling at them to get moving.

Cade and Ember entered the small, croaky carriage out of breath, sniffling as they felt another one of those things fall from the sky and shake the ground strongly.

Everything happened very fast. Before Arlette knew it, they were already on their way out of the now damaged village and looking for the nearest shelter.

Arlette's mom was crying beside her, murmuring inaudible things. She tried soothing her mother's nerves as she rubbed her tensed back in circles, whispering that they were going to be okay - that everything was going to be okay. It had to be okay.

The ride was quiet. Arlette's grandmother didn't say anything all the way through. Maybe it was all too much to process and she was still thinking about what just happened. Besides, she grew up there after all, and it being destroyed in just a minute wasn't something for the mind to easily process. Arlette pursed her lips. Ember and Cade were crying silently, taking deep breaths.

But everything was just surreal to Arlette.

She couldn't believe the fact that they had just been attacked by some unknown forces. Her village. The place where she grew up and became the person she was now. It was all too much to understand. All her family had been born and raised here.

And then there was the meadow. She knew it had lit up on fire—she could feel it. She could feel memories being burned away by the fire. Her eyes stung with tears as she pushed the burning smell and the agonizing screaming away. She didn't want to think about that now.

"Who could've it been?" Arlette's mother murmured to herself, as if she already had a deep conversation going up in her mind.

Nobody volunteered to answer. Besides, Arlette was the only one who heard her. But she didn't bother to say anything.

After about two hours, they came to a halt. And as soon as the carriage stopped, everyone hopped out as fast as they could. Arlette took her time though. She didn't know where she was - her surroundings; what awaited her—she had to become in touch with nature first.

She felt her dad's strong hands around her waist as he helped her step down carefully. Once she landed on the ground, she scanned everything mentally. Arlette was in a forest, maybe a deserted one.

"We're here," announced her father.

"What do you mean by 'we're here'?" Arlette asked, still not understanding why they were standing in the middle of a forest.

"The shelter, Arlette," her mother sighed. "This is where we're staying until we can find someplace else to settle... it's not in the best of conditions, but it's something," her mother then neared Arlette, placing her cloak's hood over her head gently, whispering in her ear, "It draws attention,"

Arlette remembered that probably because of the whole commotion, her hood had come off, because she was positive she placed it over her head the moment she heard the awful sounds coming from the sky. Still, she nodded, understanding what her mother meant.

Arlette's hair was indeed undeniably attention-drawer from what she could gather. It was a very luscious, bright, fiery red that practically allured every man and made jealous every woman. No man dared talked to her though, due to, of course, her disability. They saw it as a curse somehow - at least that's what Arlette thought they saw it as. She didn't mind though.

They entered the shelter's office, only to be told that the shelter was way too full already to accept another family.

"Are you serious?" Cade asked, annoyed. "Where are we going to stay then?"

There was silence.

"I think we all know where."

□

Once again, the carriage came to a halt, and everyone was noticeably less excited to hop out. Arlette personally felt tense. This was the last place their family had in mind to stay. It was dangerous and abnormally risky. They weren't even suppose to be near here.

Out of all places, Arlette's dad chose the palace.

"Ember, Cade, wear your cloaks," her mom instructed as they approached the gates silently. By now, Arlette's hands were trembling and she was horribly nervous, but she tried her best to hide her face under the cloak's hood—this wasn't the time for her family to see her like this. Besides, her parents were protecting her, they wouldn't let anything happen to her.

But as much as Arlette wanted to convince herself, she couldn't. It was stamped in her mind the fact that she wouldn't be completely safe staying in this place.

The guardians let them step through since they knew who her father was, and everyone gave a little bow as thanks. Arlette didn't need to bow though, she'd had her face downwards since they got here. Her mother took her hand in hers, deciding to guide her.

Being past the gates was definitely different than being behind them. The environment felt mystically magical. Arlette could hear the chirping flowers and the buzzing of the little flower fairies around them. She could smell the sweet smell of honey in the air, being delicately brushed against her face as she walked. She could also hear water splashing—maybe a fountain.

Everything just felt...magical.

Arlette was too caught up in the dreamy place that she hadn't realized her father was talking to the King until she felt an hovering power presence in front of her.

"Your Highness," there was a pause, "sorry if we're disturbing you—"

"Eric! Nonsense! You know you and your family are welcomed here always. You can call me Noel. How many times have I told you?" The King chuckled.

Surprisingly enough, the King wasn't as bad as Arlette had thought.

Arlette's dad chuckled in response, saying, "Plenty, I know," he sighed, "But I came here to ask you a favor."

"Anything, my friend," the King responded. "As long as it is not anything against the law."

"Our village has been attacked," her father paused as if leaving the sentence hanging for the King to catch on.

"Sadly, yes," inquired the King, agreeing. "I've sent the guards to look for anything that could lead to the atrocious being that did such thing."

"Yes, and so the shelter is full now," he was having a hard time trying to come up with the best words. "I was wondering if my family and I can stay until I could find somewhere else to settle. I—"

"Of course! You can stay here as long as you'd like." Said the King comprehensively. "You're all welcome. Come, come." He urged.

And they entered. Arlette was feeling worse. She gripped her mom's hand madly, trying to tell her that this was a bad idea. Very bad idea to stay in this place. It felt humongous and daunting, but yet, welcoming. And she wished, for the gods, Fate, and even karma that the infamous Prince wouldn't grace them with his atrocious presence. This just was not the time to actually come to senses if he came.

"Your daughters have grown so much, Eric." The King commented casually as they walked further and further into the huge palace.

Arlette's stomach clenched at his comment.

Oh Fate, we're in deep trouble.

---

a/n: Kind of short but I hope this was okay. Comment it makes me happy and it makes me update, and vote too! Thank you. x

- nessie xoxo

Blind Beauty | 4

SORT OF EDITED.

Chapter Cuatro

What Arlette was going through was total madness. Anger had been blooming in her chest ever since she had arrived. They weren't supposed to come here, yet they did - she just couldn't understand her parents. They could've stayed someplace else... But now that she thought of it, there had been no other place to stay but this one.

Her luck couldn't get any better, could it?

Now she was here, feeling like a prisoner, not being able to go outside or get out of her room. Regardless of the space, she was feeling sickly claustrophobic and suffocated. The emptiness of the room made her sad and miserable—she needed another living soul beside her, not just furniture and a bed. Even though her mom, dad, grandma and sisters came every day, it wasn't the same. It just wasn't.

It had been almost three weeks since they moved here, and Arlette hadn't been with another soul except, of course, her family and the maid who sometimes brought her food. She thought that living a life like this would drain her soul. She needed fresh air, the sun, the feeling of grass and flowers brush against her skin, she needed to hear the river's furious current, and to feel the dying sun in the evenings. She missed all of that so much. Too much.

Maybe it was because nature was always on her side. Nature had always helped her. It guided her and taught her. This wasn't the way she was supposed to be. She needed nature, otherwise she'd feel weak, longing, and just plain miserable.

Even though she'd tried to escape multiple times, either her parents or the guardians caught her. The first time, the guardians were the ones to catch her. She had wondered how that had even happened since they didn't know anything about her. But then she thought of her parents and what they were capable of doing if it had to do with her safety. Maybe they'd made a deal, Arlette thought, or maybe they just convinced them not to tell the King since she was just a "little, weak, blind girl" - Arlette scoffed at herself. Stop the stupid self-pity.

Arlette laid on her bed, still letting her mind go over the past events. Not much to say the least. Nothing had really happened. She shook her head. Maybe a lot happened and she didn't even know about it. She was so out of her own world, she felt as if she was going crazy. Never had she ever felt so... lost.

There was a soft knock on the door. Arlette sat up, wondering who it might be since it was way too early in the morning. Her mother's soft voice then found her ears, indicating that it was her behind the door. But Arlette stayed quiet, she didn't want to be with her mother right now. She'd been doing a good job avoiding her.

"I know you're awake, Arlette." Her mother spoke from the other side of the door.

She groaned, throwing herself back on the bed and pulling the soft blankets up to her chin and the pillows over her head as she heard her mother enter the room.

After a few seconds, she felt the bed sink a little at the place by her feet where her mother was sitting.

"Arlette," Her mother urged.

"Hmm?" She hummed, not moving.

"We need to talk," her mother said concretely.

Arlette stayed quiet, her pillows still over her head. She didn't need to talk to her mother about anything. Everything was already too clear.

Couldn't her mother understand? This wasn't her. She didn't belong here.

There was a silence. A long, almost painful silence. That is, until her mother blurted out, "He met Ember."

Arlette froze.

She sat up very slowly, pushing her disheveled hair out of her face, then faced her mother.

"What?" Maybe she didn't hear what her mother just told her, at least, not very well, she needed to hear it again.

"The Prince met Ember, Arlette. He. Met—" Arlette cut her off.

"Yes, mom, I understand what you said, it's not like I'm deaf." Arlette said, extremely frustrated with her mother. "How?" Arlette wondered out loud as she sat crossed legged, ignoring whatever her mother was going to say next about previous remark.

Her mother took a deep breath. "I-I don't know..." She mumbled quietly, "Ember said she was walking down the hallway and he just appeared out of nowhere..."

No, Arlette thought. For some reason Arlette knew Ember was hiding something. She could feel it. That was the thing about Ember. She manipulated minds and thoughts. She was able to make anyone think what she wanted them to think. She was very powerful, but she never used it against the good.

Maybe she was scared. Maybe she couldn't manipulate his mind for self defense and so she made up a story. Maybe she wasn't supposed to be in that hallway.

"Where is she?" Arlette was up and going through her closet.

"Arlette, calm down, they just met, he isn't going to marry her. He has yet to choose..."

"Can I just be with her? I need to talk to her, that's all." She said quickly, tying her dress' bow.

Arlette's mom neared her, placing both hands on either side of her shoulders, shaking her a little. "You're not going anywhere, Arlette. You're going to stay in this room until we settle things." She said strictly.

Arlette yanked herself away from her mom's grip, stumbling and almost falling back, "No," she shook her head furiously as tears threatened to fall.

"Don't you understand, mother?" She cried out bitterly, her voice cracking, "I can't live like this! We can't live like this! I'm not a prisoner. I don't need any of you to come and 'visit' me and then lock me up like I'm some kind of delinquent," her voice boomed against the tall walls. "I don't need maids bringing me food or guards protecting me. I thought it wouldn't be this bad but it's actually bizarre. Let Fate protect me, mother, not you or the guardians or dad or grandma or anyone. Fate is the best protector, or do I have to remind you again?"

Arlette was breathing sharply in and out, her fists were clenched and her jaw was set, about to explode.

"Just... let me out," she said lowly, before her mother could respond. "I just want to be with Ember."

Her mother let out a long sigh. "Okay, but you're not going anywhere else."

Arlette nodded, ignoring the stupidity of her mother treating her so coldly.

Her mom then grabbed her hand, lacing her arm through hers and walking out the door. The air was different. Fresher and less cluttered—something she wished her room was. She breathed in.

It wasn't nature, but at least it was fresher and more spacious. She let her fingertips delicately grace over the smooth wall as she walked, something she did very often.

It seemed like hours had passed until they stopped and her mother knocked on a door.

No answer.

Her mother knocked again.

Still no answer but a faint sob.

Arlette grabbed the knob desperately, yanking the door open.

She wasn't about to let her sister sob her eyes out alone.

She ran towards where she heard Ember's sob. When she was close enough, she grabbed her hand, while strong, mortifying emotions came from Ember like thick waves. Ember let out another sob, this time louder.

She was fluttering different words, and Arlette couldn't understand anything of what she was saying. Ember was a mess, that was the only thing Arlette was certain about.

"What's wrong, Ember?" Arlette asked softly.

Ember took several deep breaths to calm herself. "Nightmares," she breathed. "I-I've been having nightmares lately. Not like normal nightmares, but bizarre and monstrous nightmares." Her voice was raspy. "They've been haunting me lately, all because I 'misbehaved'." She let out another sob, letting go of Arlette's hand and instead, hugging herself.

"According to who?" Arlette asked. Tear were already stinging her eyes.

"The Prince," she whispered, her voice sounding frightened. It then hit Arlette that Ember was really vulnerable at this moment. This wasn't her usual self. Her usual self was sassy and never taking anything too seriously. What the Prince did to her was beyond horrible.

"What did you do, Ember?"

"I-I tried manipulating his thoughts..." She mumbled guiltily.

"Why? What was he doing?" Arlette was curious about the Prince's actions that brought her sister to try to do such a thing.

"Nothing. He did nothing. He was just showing interest but I didn't want it. I didn't want it and so I started manipulating his mind. He soon noticed and messed up my head and dreams."

"Arlette... I should take you back to your room. Your father and I will take care of this. Let's go." Her mother inquired, taking Arlette's hand quite hard and pulling her out of the room.

"Mom, I need to go back; Ember needs me." She said matter-of-factly, but frustration was seething out through her words.

"No. She needs some time alone so we're giving it to her."

Arlette gave up. She would deal with this later, but for now, she would make her mom think she'd be laying in her bed, about to fall asleep, when in reality she'd be far from doing any of that.

Blind Beauty | 5

Dedicated to AshleeMay for the epic banner!

HALF EDITED.

Chapter Cinco

Mumbling a goodbye to her mother, Arlette went back to bed excitedly, getting into the covers.

She waited and waited. Finally, when she heard her mother's footsteps fade, she jumped out again, going slowly and cautiously towards the door, but the excitement and anticipation was killing her, so being cautious or slow didn't really worked. She managed to get to the door quietly though, for which she was silently grateful for.

But then, for a brief moment, she heard heavy footsteps approach. That made her jump, startled. But she didn't move, she kept quiet, listening. They got stronger then. She flew straight back to bed, her heart literally wanting to come out of her rib cage.

Regardless, she listened attentively. The footsteps were getting closer. And closer. And closer. The closer they got, the more nervous Arlette felt. Was someone coming to her room? Someone she didn't know? It felt different, the presence. And despite the fact that whoever was getting closer to her door, was someone she didn't know. Yet, the presence felt powerful and dominant, like the King's. But it also felt cold and empty, something the King lacked.

Arlette drew the covers up to her chin anxiously, her breathing hard. She turned, trying to focus on who might be outside the door, but at the same time pretending to sleep.

The ponderous footsteps stopped right at her door.

Her breath was caught in her throat. For some reason, she already knew this wasn't the King. For some reason, she was scared. She had never felt this scared. And for some unexplained reason, she didn't want to know who was right at her door, she had a very certain idea of who it might be, yet, she wouldn't let her mind accept that.

She bit her lip to stop her from screaming. This wasn't the time to scream or cry.

The knob was being turned, she could hear it, and it took Arlette everything she had in her to not scream at the top of her lungs. The tension was so thick, she could've cut it with a knife.

The turning stopped— the door was locked . Arlette let out a small breath, relieved.

It was being turned again, but it stopped as if not wanting to force it open, and finally, the sound of the footsteps began to descend.

Arlette let out a long breath as soon as she heard the footsteps fade in the distance, slowly placing her hand on her chest.

Her heart was thumping hastily. And suddenly, she felt as if she was being choked. She needed to get out of here. The room felt heavy and ponderous. It soon hit her that it wasn't like that when the footsteps were approaching - in fact, it had never felt this foggy and heavy - just now, when whoever was outside the door left.

Arlette got out of bed dizzily. Her head was spinning. She had to get out of here - someone had done something to this room.

She went through her dress pocket and grabbed for her cane. Arlette couldn't feel her hands - she knew she was moving them but she couldn't feel it. For the first time, she felt lost. She didn't know where to go - she didn't know where the door or the window was.

She focused hard on the last time she felt the sunlight hit her. And then she let herself go, slowly following where she remembered the burning hot spot. She kept walking, bumping here and there with the side of the bed or the drawers. Her mind was still plainly foggy, which didn't help at all, but she continued until her hand touched the hot glass.

Arlette breathed heavily, in and out, and with all her might, tried to open the window, tried to push it up.

It didn't even budge.

Arlette sighed. This was going to be harder than she thought. She pushed it harder.

Maybe's locked.

But then again, she remembered that her mother had always left it unlocked in case it got too hot.

She graced for the lock, letting her hands run alongside the window. Finding it almost instantly, she pressed it to the side, a silent click resonating through her numb ears.

With more ease, she pushed the window open, the wind whipping against her face.

Arlette was so eager to get out of here. But before she could do anything else, she grabbed her cloak, covering herself as much as she could, and slowly climbed out the window. She didn't know how far she was from the ground. She knew she was in the first floor, but this place was humongous, so knowing how far she was, would be almost impossible.

Regardless, she put a foot down against the rocks on the wall of the palace, letting her foot lean on them.

She tried several times to see if the rocks could support her, and after a moment of leaning here and there, she found out that there was no way she could fall.. She tried to not think about the numbness she was going through. But she couldn't focus. Stubbornly, she fought through it.

It was also annoyingly windy, and her hood tried to come off multiple times. Every time it blew back, Arlette's heart picked up rapidly, making her almost lose her balance.

She was good at this though - climbing. It was one of her fortes. Which she was thankful for.

Arlette wasn't worried about the guardians, she knew they'd guard the front gates, but not this part of the palace - where she knew all the nature was. She knew that the King wouldn't like to opaque this beautiful place with the heavily armed guards. And she knew it because of the way the scents of the flowers found her nostrils and how it called her name while she climbed down and how every single one of them chirped alluringly and sweetly.

The King was a lover and admirer of nature, of course, like every Fae in the lands, and he sure showed it.

The flowers' scents and chirps made Arlette slowly come back to her senses. They wiped away the numbness in her head - a small smile found her lips and she jumped, landing smoothly on the ground.

Arlette didn't know where she was going. She just followed the smell. The soft lullabies of the trees that sung her name like they already knew her.

And then, she was engulfed by what she loved most. She felt trees and grass and flowers everywhere, tingling in her fingertips as she twirled about expanding her arms at her sides. She had missed this dearly. Arlette walked a little bit in the mists of this beauty as she touched and smelled the lovely creatures that were around her.

Nothing really worried Arlette since this was a place no one really came to visit. Due to the fact that this was the very King's. She stopped twirling. Maybe she shouldn't be here. But then again, she didn't really cared. She just wanted to be free. Even if it was just today. Arlette didn't want to worried about anything right now. Just freedom.

Harmonic bells softly rang above her head. They were whispering inaudible words, as if reminding her that she should go to Ember and talk about what had happened.

The wind picked up, blowing off her hood. She pulled it back over her head swiftly and started walking out of the place she was in.

As she walked, Arlette let her hand skim over the walls to feel for any door that might lead her somewhere near Ember. She knew she was close, she could feel her terror.

Arlette shuddered sadly, her sister was in a really bad state.

Suddenly, Arlette heard a growl...and it was close. Too close— maybe six feet away.

She stopped walking, frozen in her spot.

It growled again, closer. Arlette started to back away. It was a wolf, she could smell it. Woods and rain. It had this overpowering presence that radiated authority and dominance. The wolf gave a morbid snarl at her movements, following. Wolves in the Fae Lands were fearful and very huge creatures. One of the biggest creatures here in the lands. Arlette's stomach clenched sickly.

Almost instantly, the wolf was too close, Arlette could feel its breath all over her face. She stood there frozen. It was millimeters away from her. Her breath was caught in her throat at the realization that this humongous wolf was going to rip her to shreds.

It breathed her in, and Arlette let out a shallow gasp, followed by lonely tears. She clasped her hands over her mouth to stop herself from letting out a sob.

And then, the monstrous wolf did the unexpected.

It licked her tears.

Arlette tried to push him away, but it kept licking her face and nudging her playfully. No matter how many times she tried to push away or distract the wolf, it kept going back to her, nudging her and licking her face.

She let out a small giggle, burying her hand in his soft, endless fur. "Silly boy," she whispered, burying her face in his fur, caressing his sides lovingly. It felt better than a pillow. But the huge wolf wouldn't stop moving, it wanted to play.

"Phoenix!"

Arlette lost all focus again. She stumbled back and away from the wolf as it followed the cold, thunderous voice.

She started to back away, her instincts were desperately telling her to run.

But she didn't.

She couldn't.

Arlette felt someone near her, and she obediently bowed her head, hiding her face in her cloak as much as she could. It was him. The Prince. The most feared, morbid, and thoughtless person in the Fae Lands. Her hands turned cold with sweat as nervousness and tremendous fear crept over her.

His presence was so heavy and dark, Arlette had to swallow.

"Who are you?" He demanded, his voice was cold and blunt.

"Who I am is not of importance, Your Highness," she said softly under her hood, gesturing with a bow. "I apologize for disturbing you."

Arlette turned around, starting to walk towards the opposite direction - though she didn't know where she was going. The numbness had come back again.

He was behind her in less than a second. "Answer me," he growled only for Arlette to hear. "Who are you?"

Arlette knew she couldn't ignore a demand. Swallowing, she said, "My name is Arlette, Your Highness. I've come here with my parents due to some unfortunate circumstances," she kept her voice steady and clear under her hood.

"Turn around." He instructed.

Arlette obeyed, never showing a fragment of her face.

He stayed silent for a moment, as if thinking of something. Arlette was starting to get nervous, but she tried her best to cover it by thinking of something else.

"Take your hood off,"

Arlette's head throbbed violently. "Your Highness, I-I-I..."

"Take it off!"

Blind Beauty | 6

Please listen to the song on the side while reading this chapter, it'll make it a gazillion times better.

Chapter Seis

Arlette reluctantly did as told, her head pondering. She had to, there was no way she could get out of this one. She pushed her dark hood off her head, holding her head high towards where she heard the Prince's blunt and cold voice.

Thousands of emotions swirled around Arlette—her own. Everything was all over the place inside her. She didn't show any of that on the outside of course.

The Prince said nothing, but Arlette kept her head high and her face monotonous. This man was a beast, a cold and heartless beast whose presence could blow and batter anyone's mind. For some reason, it brought wonder and curiosity to Arlette. She managed to push it away though.

So much for controlling herself...

"Why isn't she running or screaming?" The Prince murmured to himself amusedly after what felt like centuries, but Arlette had heard him clearly. She knew exactly what he was talking about. And although she couldn't see his face, his very being was just as monstrous. Curiosity was desperately inching its way to Arlette's fingertips, but she shook it away as well. Not now...

"You're not from here." It wasn't a question, but regardless, Arlette shook her head, her vibrant waves brushing either side of her face. No words were able to come out of Arlette's mouth, this was too much for her. Her mind was foggy and there were inaudible voices whispering inside her head. Without a warning, he came closer to her, just enough for Arlette to gasp and almost jump out of her skin.

The Prince chuckled darkly, delighted at her fear and shock. He lowered his face, his lips almost brushing against her ear.

"Do you see this face?" He asked, his voice laced with disgust and anger. "Despite the very fact that it doesn't seem bother you, my presence still potently does," he laughed again maliciously, seemingly satisfied.

Arlette backed away hesitantly, fear crippling inside her veins. She was about to tell him she can't actually see his face, but before she could've utter a word out, she heard Ember's distant sobs call to her.

Rage quickly blossomed inside her as the memory of Ember's torture and vulnerability hit the mists of her emotions.

Her teeth gritted and her hands started to clench to fists ever so slightly. "What did you do to my sister?" She asked bitterly, her jaw set. Just the thought of him disturbing her sister's mind had her flaring in pure anger.

It didn't last for long though, he snaked toward her once again, grabbing her arm forcefully, "Don't you dare talk to me in that manner ever again," his voice thundered the skies and tall rock walls. Arlette whimpered silently, eyes stinging with tears. She could hear Ember sob harder, as if she was in pain. Arlette desperately tried to get free from his grasp. A tingle of grief and cold seeped its way to Arlette's heart at his touch though.

Arlette stopped struggling.

His emotions.

He was so broken. His heart was pitch black and clouded - but he had no coherent feelings whatsoever, just coldness, darkness, and regret. They stabbed Arlette. Everything was shattered. As she pressed her lips together to refrain her from letting out a scream, voices sang mournfully in her head. She tried hard to push it away. And they successfully, slowly descended.

One...

She looked up to where she figured his face was. He didn't say anything. Everything was quiet for a moment. The voices had died down. Her head stopped throbbing. And the only thing she could feel was her erratic heart and the roar of his presence. The tingle and itch in Arlette's fingertips got stronger.

This time she didn't try to push it away. She slowly moved her small hand up, internally almost regretting what she was doing, and moved it towards his face.

Two...

This was far beyond of what she should have been doing right now. She should've went and found Ember, after all, she was calling to her.

But, she didn't.

She stopped, as if asking for his permission. When he didn't say anything, she delicately proceed and softly placed her small hand on his face.

The Prince stiffened under her touch.

Three.

His skin instantly felt rough and ragged under her palm. She concentrated. Arlette could feel a deep, gory scar run diagonally between his cheekbone and neck. It felt bare - open - as if she was touching flesh. Swallowing, she ran her hands slowly over his chin and jaw. Everything felt raw, almost jagged. Arlette was fascinated.

She'd never encountered nor touched such face. She ran her hand over where she thought his nose and mouth were. Her fingertips lightly grazed its deformity and complexity. It was like a canvas—his face. And his deep scars and cicatrices were his art. Arlette could feel some type of warmth radiating from him.

So grotesque...

Yet so beautiful...

"Arlette!"

Arlette jumped, retreating her hand, and just like that, she felt a hard breeze whip across her. Her skirt and hair blew strongly about her, making her let out a choked gasp.

The Prince was gone.

She stood still, shocked.

"Arlette!"

It was her mother.

Arlette breathed heavily. Her mind was as clear as crystal.

"Arlette!"

No.

"Arlette, where are you?"

She did what was best—she ran.

□   □   □   □   □   □   □

"What were you thinking? You can't just go out like that and wander around—"

"I wasn't wandering around, mom." Arlette said, annoyed, her mom continued though, not listening to anything that Arlette was saying.

"And you climbed down the window! What if you had fallen and hurt yourself—all alone there—dying from pain—"

"But I wasn't, mom."

"Then I would have to get you to a healer - something we can't clearly afford right now!"

"Mom—"

"And you tried to run away too! Arlette, if you only knew the dangers of this palace, you wouldn't even get near that window."

Arlette let out a long, tiring breath. She wasn't about to argue with her mom, tossing and turning around while the guardians tried to get her back to her room was tiring enough. To be entirely honest, Arlette had no idea how her mom had found her. Well, the guardians did. She didn't get far, they caught her the minute she started to run.

Stupid guardians.

"Don't you ever do that again, Arlette." Her mom said with finality.

Arlette nodded wordlessly as she sat crossed-legged in the bed, softly fiddling with the hem of her skirt. She wasn't really paying attention to her mom as she talked about how the King babbles a lot about his gardens and fountains. Her mind was someplace else.

Her mind couldn't wrap around the realization that she had actually met the Prince—something which was immensely and openly forbidden in her parents' eyes.

Now that she'd thought of that, she hadn't seen his father in a couple of days. He'd most likely be killing himself and working harder so they can get somewhere decent to live. Her mom hadn't mentioned him, and she knew why. Arlette's mom avoided things she didn't like, or that weren't to her comfort. Like, talking about how her dad had been working day and night so that they could get out of the palace as soon as possible. But he, her mom, and everyone else knew it wasn't that easy. Settling in a new house was harder than anyone could think.

She hadn't heard him cough though. Which was good. He was getting better. For some reason, that made the whole situation a tad bit less complicated in Arlette's head.

"Are you listening to anything of what I'm saying?" Her mother asked incredulously.

Arlette shook her head.

Her mother sighed disappointedly, gave her a kiss in the forehead, and quietly stepped out of the room.

She knew Arlette wanted to be alone, but something in Arlette's gut told her that her mom didn't. A pang reached Arlette's heart at her selfishness. She couldn't do anything about it now though, her mother had left and locked the door behind her.

But Arlette needed some time alone. Just to think, go over, and analyze things.

Everything was so difficult though. Her mind seemed to always reach for the moment she met him in the gardens.

Nevertheless, of course it would.

His alluring complexity and maliciousness, the way his contorted emotions seeped through Arlette's skin and roamed wildly in her veins, how his presence radiated power and horrid darkness, and the way he talked to her—so cold and empty of any emotion or expression whatsoever.

He really is doomed to be alone.

And that, for some unknown and empty logic, made Arlette a bit sad.

She frowned, shaking her head. No. She shouldn't feel sad for someone like the beast. She should despise and loathe him. Not let her mind think about him. After all, he was horrible. Someone who didn't seem to care for anyone but himself—who was full of ego and pride. She won't let her mind play tricks on her.

Absolutely not.

☐   ☐   ☐   ☐   ☐   ☐   ☐

Beast's P.O.V

He paced around restlessly in the dark room, corrupted rage seething through his black, twisted veins. He took another drink, pouring it roughly into his tainted glass. Placing the glass between his ominous lips, he drank greedily, the strong and ponderous liquid burning down his throat.

It still wasn't enough.

He growled, clenching his fists in frustration as he slammed the glass against the wall beside him. Thick beads of sweat traveled angrily down his neck as he paced around ever so restlessly.

He heard a knock. "Your Highness?"

He stopped.

His wild eyes shot to the door behind him, were a little figure stood almost trembling.

"Did I allow you to come in? Get out!"

The small figure flinched frightfully, swallowing nervously, scratching his wrist as he bowed his head respectfully, "The King wishes for your very presence, Your Highness. He says it's urgent."

The beast laughed humorlessly. His bellowing and bitter laugh thundering the walls around them. The small figure flinched again, almost whimpering.

"Isn't it always?" He asked sarcastically. But he already knew what his father was going to say to him. It was always the same thing. And he was obnoxiously tired of it. Tired of him.

He took another glass from the wooden cabinet.

"Tell him I shall decide next week." He said concretely with finality, letting the guy know that he'd not meet his father tonight or tomorrow or the day after.

The guy nodded silently, quickly stepping out of the room and softly closing the wooden door behind him.

He poured some of the burning liquid in his glass, mixing it with a more conflicted one.

He concluded he'd deal with his father later. He wasn't about to hear the same speech over and over again. He was tired of it - of all of it. Instead, the beast turned around, and stepped outside into balcony, where the moon was bright, high, and beautiful. He glanced up at the sky, twinkling and glowing studded stars surrounding him.

The night was mesmerizingly beautiful.

His mind was annoyingly puzzled and,at the same time, mixed. He wasn't even supposed to feel this way. So much had happened in just one day...

He could still hear her silky voice echo hauntingly in his mind, "Time is ticking..."

.

.

.

a/n: Early update! x The soundtrack of this story is no other than Bring Me to Life by Evanescence! (song on the side) Please listen to it while reading this chapter (but I'm sure you have, I just like repeating stuff).

p.s I thought a lot about publishing the last part. Hope was worth it!

- nessie xoxo

Blind Beauty | 7

P lease listen to the song on the side.

Chapter Siete

Beast's P.O.V.

He couldn't stop.

He couldn't stop thinking about her.

Remembering the day he saw her play with Phoenix, he walked around restlessly, never forgetting her beautiful, tragic, and delicate face. So much innocence, he felt it was a sin to even think about her in the way he was thinking.

: : Flashback : :

She jumped at his bellowing voice. And he noticed the way she trembled when Phoenix left her side. She was completely covered in a cloak, and the only evidence he had that she was female was the way her cloak clung slightly tight around her waist.

He didn't know who she was, or why was she here.

Phoenix came to his side in an instant, his loose tongue hanging out of his mouth breathlessly.

The wolf eyed him pleadingly, as if asking if he could go back to the girl.

He shook his head strictly, ordering to go on the other side. The huge wolf left unwillingly, only leaving her standing there, noticeably shaking.

She knew it was him; the Beast.

It was almost laughable the thought that he was known as the Beast or the Cursed for all this dreaded years, when actually, he did have a name.

People never seemed to remember that he was actually someone—not just some morbid monster who came from the darkest of places. Yet he already felt like a monster. He was a monster. That was no problem to him. The most horrible and hideous monster to ever be born in the Fae Lands. There was no credible argument on that. And he wasn't complaining.

As he glanced at the girl, he was surprised to see that she hadn't ran or screamed yet.

But what surprised him more was the fact that the his wolf didn't do anything to her. Wolves were acid, untamable creatures, that only the most strongest and powerful could be able to own them or even be near them.

He was perplexed that she actually tended his fur.

He shook his head shortly, dismissively, and instead, started to approach the girl. As he neared her, he could see her slightly bowing her head. He heard her swallow, her excruciating nerves sailing out of her in heavy waves.

That satisfied him - power always did.

"Who are you?" he asked coldly.

Her voice was like silk.

"Who I am is not of importance, Your Highness." She said softly, pausing. "I apologize for disturbing you." And then she turned around, walking off the opposite direction like she had just not stepped into his land.

That infuriated him.

The wind whipped across her, blowing her alluring scent to his flared nostrils. That made him snake toward her faster, making her gasp as he stood dangerously close behind her.

"Answer me," he demanded as his nostrils were filled with her intoxicatingly elusive scent. He controlled himself. "Who are you?" Poisonous rage seethe through him madly as he waited for her answer.

He heard her swallow again, this time, her voice came out more clear. "My name is Arlette, Your Highness. I've come here with my parents due to some circumstances."

Arlette...

He wanted to know who this Arlette was...

"Turn around." He was trying hard to control himself.

She obeyed silently, gently turning around. Her dark cloak looked almost too big on her, but at the same time, it fitted her impeccably.

He didn't know what was happening to him, weird thoughts twirled inside him. Thoughts that had were buried a thousand feet under him, that had never surge into the surface. By now, he would've messed up with this girl's mind, like he always did. Or tell her how she shouldn't be alone in this place, and scare her off. Or call the guardians to take care of her. But he did nothing of that, and the girl didn't contribute. She seemed strong and determined under her hood. By now, he'd concluded, most girls would've faint right in front of him, or scream, or run, but the girl did nothing of that. She was different.

But of course she was, he'd noticed that since he saw her. Her vibe was quite powerful and undeniably noticeable. Not many females were that powerful in the fae lands. Not anymore.

"Take your hood off,"

He sensed her painful shock as she stammered, "Your Highness, I-I-I..."

His patience wore thin.

"Take it off!"

The girl flinched frighteningly, hesitating before completely taking her hood off.

He took a step black, briefly blinking.

He just... stared. That was the only coherent thing he could do.

He just... looked at her beautiful and delicate face, slightly heart-shaped and almost pale. Small steady nose. Crimson red, vivid and heavy waves that went down to her waist as her they started to smoothly come out of her cloak. He let his eyes graze her vibrant, dazzling green orbs that bored into his eyes as if she was almost looking through him. They twinkled, as if they were hiding something only she had the honor of finding, but he figured that she herself couldn't or perhaps wouldn't.

And as she stared right back he could only wonder one thing:

"Why isn't she running or screaming?"

He'd realized he'd said it out loud when he saw the girl's reaction - she seemed anxious.

The more he looked at her, the more her face, and in fact, her whole pose, looked foreign.

"You're not from here."

The girl shook her head softly, her waves brushing either side of her face.

: : : :

He forcibly shook the memory away as he concentrated on what his father was babbling about. It was an endless sermon about how he should choose his future wife. Deeply describing her from head to toe. Personality and characteristics. His father was never like this, he really was going mad about him getting a princess. The Prince's patience was rapidly wearing thin, and as his father noticed that, he instead invited him to eat supper with him, something they didn't do very often.

"You know I only want the best for you," his father remarked as they ate.

The best, such acid words that the only good they did to him was sink in his ominous heart, in the hypocrite way.

"The day is set," said his father, as if expecting an answer from him. But he didn't say anything, he already knew that. His father continued, "This Saturday,"

If he wanted, he could've stopped this the day his father mentioned "companion". Long ago, he would've put his father in his place—tell him that it wasn't an order to do as he wished. After all, secretly, he had much more power than him. He wasn't about to let him know that. Not in the meantime anyways.

But he wanted to try. As lunatic as that sounded, he wanted to try his fate. He had to, there wasn't much time left. She let him knew that the other night, but again, he already knew that. He'd been living like this way too long, some things can only last so long...

"Who will be there?" The Prince asked casually.

"Everybody," the King said spontaneously. "Your aunts, cousins, uncles, and of course, the taken's family."

The Prince took the bottle of wine, pouring some of its substance into his glass slowly, thoughtfully.

"So how will this work?" He asked, clarifying, "The choosing," He was trying to keep everything light. Something he was nearly forced to do.

"Simple." The King said confidently. "Take the girls, line them up, and just let Fate do the rest." He smiled broadly at his son, honesty shining in his eyes.

Fate was going to choose his princess.

"Of course," he whispered sarcastically.

But his mind couldn't help itself but suddenly remember the way that girl in the gardens grazed his distorted face. How her face changed when she touched every gore scar or cicatrix. Her fascinating and marvelous expression when she touched his lips. Her delicate and small fingers felt soft and welcoming in his skin, and her cheeks reddened from time to time, as if thinking something she shouldn't. Something about her was so difficult to explain, or sort out. She was like a puzzle—he figured that the moment he saw her.

He just hoped Fate knew what she was doing.

☐

☐

Arlette's P.O.V

Days—probably weeks—had passed by and Arlette still wasn't able to come out of her room.

Today though, the King decided to gather all of them for supper.

Arlette's stomach could only twist with anticipation.

Her mom was a nervous wreck, acting twitchy and weird. But all of them knew this day was coming so Arlette didn't know why her mother was being so dramatic and over the top. She'd always been that way though. Acting as if the world was going to shatter into pieces if nothing went the way she wanted it.

Her father and grandma were already downstairs waiting for them to come down.

Arlette's mother stepped out of the room first, accompanied by Arlette, Cade, and Ember. Today, none of them were wearing a cloak, but pretty dresses.

Arlette felt uncomfortably exposed without her cloak. She wasn't used to use it so often before, but now, it was almost a part of her.

Ember came closer to her, whispering, "I'm getting better."

Arlette didn't know why Ember was telling her that, or why suddenly she felt as if Ember was getting closer to her. Ember had never told Arlette how she was feeling or anything of the sort, not after all these years anyways. So much had changed between the three of them that she really missed that.

Arlette smiled, turning and hugging Ember tightly, "I'm glad, Ember, I am." She whispered back, her voice breaking just a little. And she really was. She was pleased to know that she was getting better, even if it wasn't by much.

They went through the hallway and down the stairs. But before Arlette went a step down the stairs, she grabbed for her cane, only for Ember to grab her hand and stopping her from doing so.

"I'll take you," she said, lacing her arms through hers, and slowly stepping down the stairs.

"Thank you," said Arlette quietly.

The four of them went down the stairs, roaming another set of long hallway and then stopping.

Everything happened too fast for Arlette to function properly.

"Hope you enjoy yourselves, ladies," she heard a deep voice say—probably a guardian.

Arlette soon heard an oak door being open, it groaned and protested as doing so. She took a deep breath.

Arlette wondered if the Prince was here.

"Oh, ladies!" Cheered the King, as Arlette heard a chair scrape against the floor. "You've come to finally join us. Do please take a seat."

"We're sorry for the delay," started her mother as they walked toward them, but was politely cut off by the King.

"No need to apologize, supper's still on its way," and then he added, "You all look very lovely."

They all said thank you in unison, each one of them slowly taking a sit. Her grandma and dad greeted them.

"I want you all to meet one of my sons," said the King. "This is Aaron,"

Arlette's heart thumped madly in her chest.

But it wasn't him.

She knew that. But she still wanted to make sure.

So he had a brother?

"Good evening, ladies," Aaron paused. "you all look very beautiful,"

He talked with such... passion. There wasn't any other way to put it. It was like his words meant everything. It was honesty—she figured that. Arlette felt like he was talking straight at her as he introduced himself. She could feel his eyes on her. She didn't know how, but she could. She could feel his eyes boring into her, almost making her sink in. But it wasn't the bad way. He radiated this warmth and royalty that it was actually nice to be around him, She smiled politely from time to time when he made a joke about the horses.

After finishing eating, they just sat talking aimlessly.

Arlette was talking to Ember.

"You haven't seen him?"

"Not since that day, no," said Ember. "It's like he controls it. Because some days, I can't even get off bed. But other days, I feel like nothing had happened. It's making me feel tired."

Ember must've looked—and felt—like literal crap.

"You should get some rest then. Since your head is so unsettled, it's better to get some rest." Arlette didn't know what else to tell her, she had never encountered anything like this.

"But I'm scared to dream, Arlette. I'm scared to even think, because it always comes back."

Arlette felt Ember get up from her chair. She grabbed her arm gently, stopping her, "Wait—where are you going?"

"I need some fresh air," Ember said monotonously, getting out of Arlette's grip.

Arlette sighed, letting her go.

After a couple of minutes, she decided to listen to her mother talk about the village. It was comforting, really, to hear her talk about the village with such pride.

Arlette felt someone grab her hand gently. She gasped at the sudden gesture, only to be followed by Aaron's rich voice. "It's a pleasure to meet you, miss," he kissed her hand softly, his lips warm and soft.

She felt her pale cheeks reddened as she said, "Please call me Arlette," she smiled to hide the redness.

He tasted her name on his lips. "Arlette..." he paused. "Would you mind taking a walk with me?"

He was asking Arlette for a walk?

She hesitated, "M-my dad—"

"I already asked for his permission," he said. She could feel the smile on his face.

Arlette was a bit surprised, no one had ever showed such interest in her.

When she didn't say anything, Aaron proceed, "I'll take that as a yes."

Not really functioning what was happening, she stood up slowly, letting Aaron guide her outside in the husky night.

Blind Beauty | 8

Chapter Ocho

Aaron was most likely the most kind, charming, and courteous man Arlette had ever met. He was so funny, Arlette constantly grabbed onto her sides and wiped her tears from laughter. He made the lamest of jokes, but that's what made them funny, and Arlette was just about to die with him.

After several moments of crazy laughter (and calming herself), she felt good. Arlette hadn't had a good laugh since she could remember. All she can remember were worries. There were happy times, but they were masked with the constant worries. She always tried to see the bright side to everything though, which often almost worked.

"I must say, Arlette, you're so bewildering," said Aaron amused, but quickly added, "Not in a bad way, though. But in the beautiful and delightful way. In the way that makes you want to know more, and at the same time, be more confused."

She couldn't really understand what he meant. Arlette didn't found herself that interesting. But the way he said it, proved her wrong. He seemed to find her very interesting.

The Prince too, stupid. Remarked a voice at the back of her mind, making her reluctantly remember.

But the thought was pushed back when she heard Aaron talk.

"I heard what happened to your village." Said Aaron, more calmly now. He had stopped laughing and making jokes, his voice turned pleasant and serious, showing the deep importance he felt for Arlette's village.

They had also stopped walking.

Arlette nodded slowly, her expression changing as she bowed her head a little. So much memories had been burned and shattered away, the thought itself made her feel a pang deep in her heart, making her eyes sting a little with tears. She pushed them away, but they were there—she could feel them. Her lips quirked up into a small, sad smile, "Some say things happen for a reason…" Aaron took her cold hand gently as she continued to talk, more shaky now, "So perhaps we have to accept them."

"Not always," said Aaron softly. "Some accept them because they have to, because Fate doesn't give them another option. Instead of getting passed the pain, they live with it, not even noticing, and not ever accepting the fact that something that was so precious to them is suddenly gone." His fingers touched her cheek as the wind blew her hair away. He was trying to make her understand that it was okay to feel this way. And that, just that, made her feel a little bit better.

"I miss it," whispered Arlette, so much, it hurts.

Aaron engulfed her in a warm, soothing embrace then. He hugged her tightly, not saying anything. Arlette didn't contribute either, so she just buried her face in his chest as small tears started to fall.

It was so comforting to be in his arms, she didn't want to let go. It was like he wanted to take away all her pain in that embrace. Like he was letting her hand him all her worries, and he accepted them easily.

His emotions were so potent, she could identify every single one of them easily. But they were all in a mist, floating in a foggy cloud up at the top of her head.

Soon, realization dawned into her, making her pull away hesitantly, embarrassed. How could she get that close. That was close. Too close. She didn't know him. "I-I'm so s-sorry, I shouldn't h-have—"

"Shh.." He hushed softly, coming closer to her. "I'm the one who should be apologizing, Arlette." He chuckled softly as he gently grabbed her chin. The way her name rolled off his tongue made her feel some way that she herself couldn't identify. Arlette felt herself blushing spontaneously hard. He was so close...

It was getting cold and she didn't have her cloak. The wind whipped coldly against her face once again. She felt Aaron's face dangerously close to hers. And for a moment, Arlette's heart stopped. She could feel his warm breath fan her face. By now, Arlette must've looked like a tomato. She gasped quietly, making her heart thump hard in her chest. She tried. Arlette tried not to close her eyes...but she couldn't. She couldn't help herself no to, so she, slowly, fluttered them closed even though it wouldn't make a difference.

She didn't know if she was doing the right thing by closing her eyes. Arlette had very little experience whatsoever, but she guessed she learned that from her sisters. They always talked about what you should do when a male comes that close to you. Arlette always listened to their conversations, because she was curious. But we all know what they say, right? Curiosity killed the cat.

But Aaron didn't do what Arlette thought he should do. Instead of placing his lips on hers, like she thought he should do, he placed them very softly down her jaw. Arlette quickly let out a small, surprised gasp, but Aaron didn't stop. He ran alluring, soft kisses down her neck, stopping at the crook of her neck, and breathing her in. Arlette had never experienced this. She felt weird but at the same time... nice. So nice.

She heard the leaves of the trees rustle restlessly, making her throw back her head a little. Aaron touched her lower back, pushing her closing to him. Arlette drew a breath. She didn't also understand why she was giving in so easily, but it was just so hard not to.

"So beautiful..." he whispered breathlessly against her neck.

Cool shivers ran up Arlette's spine. She was telling herself to pull away. That this wasn't going to end good. Not with him complimenting her the way he just did.

Just when she was about to pull away, when realization and something more hit her, she heard something—someone growl. A sick, nasty growl that was just too familiar to not recognize. The air had suddenly changed, it became thick and numb, ponderous also.

But maybe Arlette was going crazy. She hadn't had been thinking about the Prince as much as she had use to the past few days. Aaron got her mind off things. Off him.

But Arlette wasn't going crazy. Aaron stopped as soon as he heard the growl, then he seemed to look up where he heard it, which was several feet behind Arlette. He didn't say anything.

She stayed mortified in place, but Aaron swayed her extremely fast, invisibly, behind him, shielding her from whatever was growling. But they both clearly knew who it was, everybody just seemed to avoid it until something actually happened.

"What are you doing here?" Aaron's voice turned cold and venomous, like his. Almost like his.

And that was when Arlette realized the Prince wasn't in dinner earlier that evening.

She felt him approach Aaron, and she slowly hid herself even more behind his back, feeling overwhelmed and numb.

The Prince chuckled bitterly, "I see you got yourself company." He was closer to Aaron now.

Something was telling Arlette that he had been watching all along. And just that, made her stomach twist and her head pound.

"I don't think that's any of your business. Father has been looking for you, I'd suggest you go," Aaron's voice was noticeably, frighteningly, less cold.

"You're not going to introduce me to the lucky lady?" There was something in his voice that was so hard to identify...

Arlette's heart wanted to come out of her rib cage.

"Just go," Aaron suddenly sounded tired.

"Do you think that low of a woman?" The Prince asked boastfully.

And then it hit Arlette.

Every time Aaron rejected, he was getting, or being, drained—probably physically and emotionally—by him. And he knew that. He just didn't want the Prince to see her, when in fact, they had actually met before. Arlette felt horrible.

She touched Aaron's arm gently, making him turned around to face her, and then she whispered, only for him to hear, "He's only asking you to introduce me... how bad can it get?"

Arlette was doing this for Aaron, she didn't want him to feel sick, or whoever knows what, just because of that.

Aaron sighed, staying silent for a moment, and then, finally, turned around again, this time with Arlette's hand enlaced in his arm.

Aaron was really a shield for her, because the moment Aaron turned around with her, heaviness attacked her.

She immediately felt the Prince get closer to her. He grabbed her hand gently. Kissing it tenderly, he stroked her knuckles. Head bowed, Arlette drew back a shocked breath. His hands were big and rough, slightly warm. She could feel his eyes on her the whole time. She felt her pale cheeks redden. His touch quickly stirred some of his emotions. Arlette could stroke the tingle of amusement, anger, pain, and infinite darkness that crawled up her arm.

He had never been this gentle to her. But then again, she'd only been near him once. Not that that gives out anything of him being anywhere near nice to her or anyone in that manner.

"I'm the Prince of the palace and Fae Lands. It is a delight pleasure to meet you..."

"Arlette." Aaron finished.

"Arlette," said the Prince. But he already knew that.

He let go of her hand and she no longer felt his stirring gaze on her, but stayed in place. "I see that she's not yours yet,"

"I just met her today," said Aaron matter-of-factly, mockingly, like the Prince.

"Perfect," murmured the Prince, only to himself, but Arlette heard him. She could. After all, her senses were much higher than anyone else's.

She wished she couldn't have heard him.

"You should go. It's tonight. Father's waiting for you." Aaron said, clearing his throat.

Arlette wondered if the prince had thought about her like she had thought about him.

"That's true. I must go." And then he was gone—just like that. Arlette gasped as the wind whipped across her.

Soon enough, Arlette felt nauseous and dizzy. Aaron grabbed her around the waist, before she could stumble and fall. "Are you alright?"

His words rang noisily in her head as numbness and sickness attacked her.

Perfect. Perfect. Perfect. Perfect. Perfect. Perfect.

What did he mean by that?

And then Aaron's voice.

It's tonight. Tonight. Tonight. Tonight. Tonight. Tonight. Tonight. Tonight.

Too much coincidence.

Too much coincidence. Coincidence. Coincidence. Coincidence. Coincidence.

Feeling a hard pang inside her head, Arlette let out an agonizing scream. Her knees trembled madly as she felt like her mind was being stabbed continuously. She felt Aaron pick her up before her knees gave out, walking quickly without a word. Distorted and twisted voices rang too loudly in her head, slamming forcefully against it. She tasted the metallic, bitter taste of blood in her tongue.

"Aaron!" She screamed torturously as another pang hit her thoughts.

Aaron was running now. "Hold on. Just hold on a bit more, Arlette." His voice showed pure despair.

Hot, streaming tears ran down her face. "It hurts…" she sobbed.

"I know it does, Arlette," Aaron said quietly, helplessly. "Just hold on."

Once again, she felt the blistering, screeching pain bang and cut against the walls of her thoughts, dry and nasty growls invading it.

"Aaron!" Arlette shrieked, noticeably less stronger now. She was losing strength.

"Stay awake, Arlette. Stay awake." Aaron ordered. But she couldn't, she wasn't strong enough. It was too much. She had never experienced such acid pain in her life.

Arlette was panting, letting the numb darkness drag her in—drag her to peace.

The last thing she heard was Aaron screaming for help as he collapsed on the floor with her.

□   □   □

Aaron's P.O.V

"So she's alright now?" He asked.

The healer nodded, looking around at the silent family, then letting his eyes land on the beautiful, sleeping Arlette, "She just needs some rest for tonight. If I am right, by tomorrow, she should be like new." He paused, "Whoever did that to her left her physically and mentally drained to the maximum. However, she's strong. If that were to happen to any of us, we would have to rest for at least two weeks." He looked at Aaron now. "She is truly gifted."

Aaron nodded approvingly, then said, "Thank you so much, Cruz."

"No need to thank me, sir. This is what I do." He smiled broadly, bowing.

Later on, Cruz excused himself, only leaving Aaron with Arlette's family.

As he glanced at them, sitting beside her bed, he ran his hand over his dark hair, sighing guiltily, "I am so sorry for not protecting Arlette the way I should... I swear I did my best—"

"We know, son." Her father said, looking at him. "You were under his silent command so you couldn't do anything to avoid the way he shattered her mind." He got up and approached Aaron, "But I will forever be in depth of you for bringing her back to us safely." He hugged Aaron, and he returned it gratefully. "Thank you. For saving my daughter,"

They pulled away, and Aaron said, "You don't owe me anything, sir. I would've done it a hundred times if I had to." He paused then glanced at Arlette, then at her father expectantly. "May I?"

Her father nodded. "Of course," then stepped aside.

Aaron shortly bowed his head, thanking him, then, approached the sleeping Arlette, standing right beside her. He felt a chair scrape against the floor behind him. Looking over his shoulder, he saw a pale girl with brunette curls and striking blue eyes standing beside the empty chair. She smiled at him, offering the chair, then turned around walking quietly out of the room.

He noticed that her grandmother and father had stepped out of the room too, only leaving him with her mother and another girl, most likely her sister.

He took the chair quietly, setting it close to her bed. He sat, slowly taking her cold, delicate hand. As he looked at her, it was sickly to see that she had gotten abnormally pale. Too pale. But she was still as beautiful as ever. With her fiery waves sprawled beautifully around her pillow. Pastel pink lips, now almost purple from the paleness...

He kissed her knuckles, cold against his lips. "I'm so sorry, Arlette," he whispered, his eyes looking downward.

He knew it wasn't going to end well the moment he saw him. Aaron should've run.

He knew he'd leave a mark. He always did.

Pure rage grew inside Aaron. He was going to pay. His brother was going to pay for what he did to Arlette.

Tomorrow night, after the choosing.

He will pay.

Aaron got up, kissing Arlette on the forehead, stepping out of the room as quietly as he could.

The decision was made.

Blind Beauty | 9

C hapter Nueve

It was cold, too cold perhaps.

Arlette was walking. She didn't know where to. She was just... walking.

But it was too cold. She'd never experienced nothing like this. Her whole body was in miserable pain. Her lungs trembled and wept for warmth. Her skin prickled murmurs with the cold as her veins filled with what felt like frosted water. It ran and stomped in her veins vigorously, making her wince and screech. Her delicate fingers were twisted and wobbly and dead from the cold. They hurt. A lot. Her bones crawled, cutting and clinging to herself as the cold stroke them sickly. She fell to the bitter floor, her bare knees hitting it with full force. She let out a cry, clenching to her side and grabbing her knees painfully, helplessly, as her fingers were no use.

A raw, icy wind picked up, making her purple-pale lips let out another screeching cry for help.

Arlette didn't know how much time she stayed there, but she was between unconsciousness and reality, going and coming, coming and going.

She told herself that it was better to stay in between than in unconsciousness. She had no idea what place was this.

But through the midst of it, she heard numb footsteps approach.

That made her cry for help even more. But it her cries were gone with the wind, making her sob faintly in frustration.

Where was she?

But then she heard the footsteps approach her. They were quick and short.

They stopped, right in front of her. They didn't do anything, as if just enjoying the view.

There was something that surprised Arlette, and that was their presence. It was empty and arrogant, selfish and self-absorbed, also dark and poisonously evil.

Still, she was dying, and she needed help.

"P-Please... help me." She croaked, painfully extending an arm towards whoever was in front of her.

There was silence.

But then—

"And why should I?" It was a female—that was the first thing that Arlette realized. Her voice was hard and dominant but at the same time silky, beautiful. A mix of emotions. For some reason, Arlette felt that this girl knew her. But how come she didn't? She heard the woman pace cautiously, slowly, around Arlette, as her heels clacked obnoxiously against the frozen floor. "You know, it's funny how most of the fae wish coming here..." The woman mused cruelly.

"W-where am I?" Arlette's voice was dry, distant.

The woman had stopped pacing around her. She laughed impudently. Not a giggle, but a booming, hysterical laugh, as if Arlette had just told her the most funniest joke in the history of existence.

If Arlette wasn't dying from the cracking cold, she swore she would've slap the continuous cracklings out of her obnoxious laugh.

Several moments had passed until she could compose herself. "I'm sorry," she said through fading laugher, not really meaning it. "You're just really funny,"

The woman took a couple of breaths. "Anyways, what was I saying?" She paused. "Oh, right. You don't know where you are?" She giggled. "Oh boy, so naive." The woman crouched down Arlette's level. "You're in the outside world, darlin'." She whispered, followed by another set of hysterical laughter. Arlette didn't say anything. It hadn't really sunk in yet.

"Want me to tell you what the outside world is, too?" She asked laughing.

So she was in the outside world... But what she doing there? What'd happened?

"Why is it so cold then?" Arlette asked through gritted teeth, ignoring the woman's arrogant question. She felt like she was losing herself again.

"Sweetheart, it's winter. It's supposed to be cold." The woman said matter-of-factly, boastfully.

Before Arlette could utter a word out, she heard a snap, quickly, startlingly, changing the environment into a hot and cozy one. Arlette's lungs were quickly filled with familiar warmth and gentleness, and the ice in her skin started to melt.

She breathed in profoundly, letting the warmth caress her skin and bones, letting her fingers come to their normal selves.

Arlette sat up from the smooth, carpeted floor, rubbing her hands together.

"Better, huh?"

They were in a house. The woman's voice sounded distant, somewhere in it.

Arlette nodded.

The woman came back. "Come on, get up." She took hold of Arlette's hand and pulled her up effortlessly, pushing her and sitting her on the sofa.

She heard the woman pull a chair in front of Arlette and sitting down.

Arlette could feel the woman's piercing eyes burning into her soul as silent moments passed by. Arlette was starting to feel extremely uncomfortable. She didn't know why she was here, or who was this woman, or why had she taken her here. But finally, quietly, amusedly, the woman said, "So you're what has been roaming his mind lately." She stayed quiet again, but then said, "Hmm, not bad." She chuckled venously.

"W-whose m-mind?" Arlette stuttered, somehow not wanting to know the answer to that question.

"Oh, aren't you just a little ray of sunshine!" The woman clapped once, and Arlette winced. She was too loud. "Maybe you should figure that out by yourself."

"Who are you?" Arlette asked. Maybe she could get a clue as to why all of this was happening. She felt very little and insignificant in this woman's presence.

"I was starting to wonder when were you going to ask." She sighed. "Darlin', but if I tell you, this won't be no fun. The game has just started!"

Her voice was so creepily excited that it frightened Arlette. Whatever game this woman was going to play would definitely be no fun.

She just wanted to go home.

The woman was saying something, but Arlette couldn't understand anything of what she was saying. They were murmurs and large wisps of loudness at the same time, resonating through the house then her whole body. She heard some screeching, harsh sound coming from her head, it was taunting, letting its familiarity make itself present.

Arlette put her palms on either side of her temples. "No, no, no, no, no, no," she begged, "not again, please..."

But it didn't matter how many times she begged, it would always come back.

Once again, the familiar, excruciating pain came back, cutting and slashing through her thoughts and mind. Arlette let out a strangled scream as pangs and thorns pierced through her head.

The environment was flipping back and forth, from hot to cold, cold to hot. Arlette gritted her teeth, trying to fight the stinging pain. She could hear thousand of fingernails dig themselves deep on chalkboards. Her fists clenched the arms of the sofa, and once again, she was losing herself. The darkness was dragging her in. She tried to fight it, she truly did. But it was too much, she'd never be able to fight it off.

Someone was grabbing her, shaking either side of her shoulders. She tried to pull away, yanking and tossing herself away, screaming.

"Arlette, calm down! It's just me!" Her mother shouted, trying to stop her.

Arlette slowly stopped. She was back - she was back to the palace. Happiness blossomed inside her. Arlette sat up. The pain in her head had vanished.

"Arlette, you're shaking," her mother mumbled, then quickly hugged her. "It was just a bad dream. You're safe now." She paused as they pulled away. "How are you feeling?"

"Good." Arlette answered, smiling. She was feeling more than good. She was feeling amazing—like new.

"That's great, sweetheart," her mother hugged her again, murmuring, "Thank the lords that boy saved you."

"Who?"

"Aaron..."

And then Arlette remembered.

"Aaron..." Arlette repeated.

"Yes, Aaron."

Arlette pulled away. "Where is he?"

"He's..." She paused, "Arlette you should get ready."

She frowned. "Why? Where am I going?"

Her mother sighed. "You're..." she hesitated. "participating in the choosing... along with your sisters," Arlette heard her mother swallow, and she could tell that she was trying not to cry in front of her.

This was the one thing they were avoiding.

Arlette didn't know what to say. "But mom—"

"'But mom' nothing, Arlette. It's done. The king ordered us to." Her voice was monotonous, miserable. "We all knew it was inevitable anyway. Just go and take a quick bath, the maid already handed me your dress."

Arlette crossed her arms over her chest. She hated how her mother was giving up so easily.

"I'm not going anywhere," she said stubbornly.

Her mother let out an exhausted sigh, "Please, Arlette, don't make this harder than it already is. I've got enough just with the thought that any of you three could be the chosen one." She took her Arlette's hand, dragging her out of the bed. "Just please go take a bath. I'll help you get ready."

Arlette couldn't believe this. "What about Ember and Cade?"

"They're ready." Said her mother as she untied Arlette's dress bow hurriedly. Arlette could feel her mother shaking, getting frustrated as she tried to unlace the dress' long laces.

Arlette knew that this must've been really hard for her mom. "Mom just—" Arlette turned around holding her mother on either side of her shoulders, "Just calm down, okay?"

Her mother took a deep breath, and Arlette touched her face gently. She touched tears.

Arlette's heart clenched, and she could feel tears in her eyes forming. "It's going to be okay. Just pray, okay? I'm not the only one who's going to be there. There'll be dozens of different girls, too." Arlette smiled through her twinkling tears.

"I know, I just—"

Arlette interrupted her, "Shhh... Just go rest until I get out of the bath-room," she turned her mother around, gently pushing her towards the bed, "you sound exhausted."

Her mother didn't argue, and Arlette took this opportunity to quickly take her clothes off and step into the bathroom.

Arlette took her time—she didn't want to disturb her mother. As she washed her hair, she let her mind wander, of everything that had happened. How her mother told her to wear a cloak the days she went out to the meadow in the beginning of this tangled knot. Or how she had told her to always wear her hood because her hair constantly drew attention. Or when her mother went full on extreme and decided to lock her in her room, and most likely talked to the guardians about her situation...

It was all useless, all those things went in vain. Even if they wanted it or not, this was going to happen, and all of them knew that, but they just wanted to try. After all, it doesn't hurt to try, does it?

But then that dream... That painfully vivid dream.

It felt so real, so incredibly and agonizingly real.

Arlette could remember everything, especially the woman's last words before everything just went numb, "Darlin', but if I tell you, this won't be no fun. The game has just started!"

She felt sick every time she heard that woman's voice.

'The game...'

What game?

Finally, with a shudder, Arlette stepped out of the bathroom, taking a small towel and wrapping it around herself protectively.

She slowly made her way to the door, taking the knob and twisting quietly. Opening the door, she stepped out of the bathroom and into the room.

"Why'd you take so long?" Her mom complained.

Arlette sighed, drying herself, ignoring her. A couple of seconds later, her mother handed her some undergarments. And as she put them on, she asked, "Where're Ember and Cade? Why aren't they here?"

"Oh, Arlette, again with the questions..." Her mother sighed. "They didn't want to come."

Her mother threw the dress over her head, as Arlette asked, "But why?"

She didn't answer and instead, started to adjust the dress, slightly pulling it down. Arlette knew her mother wasn't going to answer that question, so instead, she changed the subject, "Is dad going to be there?"

"All of us are going to be there," she answered as she tied the laces effortlessly.

Arlette stayed silent. She knew it was for the best.

After her mother finished adjusting her dress, she did Arlette's make-up, neither of them uttering out a single word. The silence wasn't awkward, it was a comforting, soothing silence. A silence that wouldn't want to be disturbed. A silence that could even be a good friend—a companion.

Everything happened really fast, and that was what Arlette hated—when she was too dazed off to even really function what was happening. But she remembered it all pretty well.

Ember, Cade, and herself walked down the stairs, along with their mother, walking an endless hallway soon met by a big door.

Arlette's heart bumped hard against her chest, her breathing was hard. As she slightly clenched her hands into fists, she could feel the cold sweat peeling off of them. She sent a small prayer up the heavens, first thanking fate for all she had offered and given her, and then wishing everything will go okay, and that the Prince's eyes will fly pass the three of them. Arlette swallowed the lump in her throat as the guardian wished them good luck, and soon, maybe too soon, the door was being open.

.

.

---

a/n: I want to thank you all for patiently waiting for the chapter when the choosing will take place. (It will be in the next chapter, btw!). Lol. So thank you. Just wait a bit more. Until next update!

- nessie xoxo

p.s Check out the banner in chapter seven. I LOVE it!

p.s.s If you're reading this, Zoe, I promise you, in the next update! You know what I'm talking about ;)

Blind Beauty | 10

Just look at that beautiful banner on the side... It's my new favorite. There's no words to describe how much I love it. Also, the song on the side. As usual, please listen to it to get you on the mood (and it basically explains everything so please, yeah, listen to it). ;) Dedication goes to my lovely Zoe for it. <3

Chapter Diez

Beast's P.O.V.

"I feel bad for you," she said, her mischievous eyes twinkling as the moon swayed over them. She was wearing a black, highly elegant dress, with rather too high heels. And her face was heavily made up. Her voice was so angelic, he almost believed her. Almost.

Rage was erupting off of him like fireworks. He tried to calm himself, but all he wanted to do at this exact moment was to grab her and twist her neck until she was no longer breathing. Feelings couldn't even describe the pure hatred he had for this woman standing a few feet away from him, evilly looking like a goddess.

He tried to talk as light as he could.

He almost laughed out loud at the word "light".

It felt quite weird for his lips to sculpt her name out, "Simone, I know there's no much time left—"

"Oh! Have you just noticed, my dear?" She remarked sarcastically, her voice obnoxiously loud. "There hasn't been much time left since the beginning of the century."

The beast growled as the trees overhead rustled restlessly. The woods were quiet, dark, with only the moon sliding through the trees. She came closer, walking slowly around him, her finger tracing his skin. Her soft black dress blew in the wind. Her touch was dark, sickening. He was tired of her. Of her games.

He could see her flinch as he growled, fear in her eyes. But it disappeared as soon as it came.

Her darkness was as overbearing as his. Too much, too suffocating; claustrophobic. But it didn't bother him, of course. He was darkness itself.

She didn't even flinch at his abnormal anger, as if she was used to seeing him this way. She stopped and stood eye level with him as his nostrils flared. Her big doe eyes grazed over his contorted, twisted face. It didn't seem to bother her. She just looked at him, almost proudly. As if she was proud of the masterpiece she had done. She put a soft, cold hand in his cheek, and he could see her black, penetrating veins, going from her forearm to her knuckles. They contrasted with her pale skin, making her look almost dead.

He had the same ones.

Only in his whole body and much more potent, big, and sick.

Her hands then went down to his chest gracefully, and he tried with all his might to not rip her into shreds. If only he could kill her, but he couldn't. He couldn't understand what she was doing though.

She suddenly grabbed the collar of his attire tightly, breathing heavily, then suddenly ripped it apart savagely, vigorously. It made a scraping sound, resonating through the whole forest. It happened too fast, almost comically, but nothing about it was. The rest of the shirt slid down the floor, leaving him with his middle section naked. And then he understood.

"See this?" she asked, pointing a the big, pumping veins going all the way across his chest and all his middle section. He didn't say anything, he just stared at the familiar red, thick veins going all over his body, emotionless. They made something… A tree.

The tree was big, red, and leafless. The red, thick veins scrambled together in thick lines at the bottom was the trunk, and they went up in slightly chunky wisps of veins, stopping on his collarbones. "The red means you have very little time," her cold fingers ran over them. He flinched. "And you know that." Her lips quirked up in an evil smile. She narrowed her eyes slightly. "The signs are telling me that you have specifically a little over three weeks." She nodded, seemingly satisfied. "That should be enough."

His eyes widened, and Simone turned away walking the opposite direction. He quickly grabbed her arm turning her forcefully toward him. His eyes bored into her, "That's not enough," his voice was hoarse, dangerously low. "I need more time. You have to give me more time," he pressed.

She struggled to get away from his dead grip as she uttered out, "I can't alter it, my dear," her voice was pure venom, "If the curse isn't broken at three weeks time, you and your father are gone. There is no other way out." Tears prickled in her eyes as she was still struggling to get away, and then he realized how badly he was hurting her. He quickly let go of her arm, stepping back. She smiled at his realization. "I see that you haven't forgotten."

Simone rubbed her arm softly. There was a huge, extremely disturbing purple, green-ish mark against her pale skin. It looked thoroughly nause-ating. As she rubbed the smashed skin, its colors disappeared, along with the slightly deformity of her arm.

She then approached him slowly, her wicked, dark eyes boring into his. Standing dangerously close, she whispered, "Tick tock, tick tock…" She laughed viciously, clapping as she stepped away, quickly being swallowed by the trees.

□   □   □   □   □   □   □

Arlette's P.O.V.

"The Prince is going to choose me!"

Someone scoffed at her remark.

And then someone said, "No he's not. He wouldn't want a quite bulky girl to be with him. "

"Oh, please. Haven't you seen all these girls? They're all hideous." One of the girls whispered, and then said, rather wistfully, "Can't you just imagine? Sitting there in the throne, ruling over the Fae…" she sighed dreamily, "that would be a dream come true."

Arlette wanted to throw up.

Were these girls on some humorless spell or something?

They must've been. How on the Lords' name would someone want to be doomed for the rest of their life? It didn't make any sense to Arlette. These girls only wanted the power of being a princess and being able to rule all over the Fae Lands. That must've been it. Don't they know that all the Prince has done is bad? He's selfish, capricious, vicious... There's really no coherent words to describe him, and all these girls can think about is the throne?

Arlette thought more deeply about it. Maybe they were taught something else. After all, not all villages were the same. Maybe they had a different idea about being with the Prince. Maybe their beliefs were different, very different from Arlette's. But we all know which one is right.

These girls were brain-washed.

All of them were standing in a horizontal line, facing the throne. Arlette was somewhere between the many girls, who were bickering and whispering mundane thoughts. Weren't they all suppose to be scared out of their lives like Arlette was? Arlette was starting to wonder if she was the only one who was nerve-wrackingly frightened. Her hands were sweating and her head was pounding loudly, soft whispers telling her inaudible stuff. The guardians had tracked all their names and ages down, something Arlette found rather too creepy.

She didn't know where her family was, they separated as soon as they entered.

As they waited for the Prince to arrive, she heard footsteps coming from the far right. A majority of the girls quieted down, probably wondering who was approaching them. Seconds later, Arlette could hear the guardian's voice approach, saying, "When the Prince enters, all of you are expected to bow your heads," his voice was flat, monotonous. "You, in no means, are allowed to pick your head up if you're not ordered to."

He stopped briefly in front of Arlette as he was pointing to her, and then soon started walking again, "And you shouldn't say a word until you're ordered to." Arlette swallowed, remembering the day she met him. The guardian strided back down again, saying, rather more proudly now, "Also, since you all know Fate's mysterious ways, Fate will deliberately tell the Prince who is the one for him. Do not fret, my dears, it could be any of you." He paused. "The Prince will be here in a few minutes, so I suggest you to stay quiet."

And then he was gone.

Arlette let out a breath she hadn't realized she was holding and swallowed again. The girls started talking once again, but more carefully now, murmuring how excited they were. Arlette sighed. What was up with these girls?

And where were Ember and Cade? Arlette hadn't heard from them since they took their places in the different positions while in the line. She wondered if Ember was okay. If all of this that was happening was okay for her, or at least decent. Arlette didn't want Ember to have a nervous breakdown in front of everybody, much less the Prince. It would be total and utter chaos.

So instead, Arlette concentrated on sensing how she was feeling - find out how she was. It was hard with the many bursting, exciting, and anxious emotions going on in the endless line, but Arlette concentrated as hard as she could, shutting down any other emotions and concentrating on Ember's.

Ember's head was thrashing, uncomfortable with the constant, irrelevant emotions going on. Arlette gasped. The girls beside her quieted down and paused as if looking at her wearily. Arlette quickly looked down, embarrassed about her outburst. But thankfully, seconds later, the girls went back to their own business, and Arlette couldn't believe what she had just witnessed. She could get into people's mind?

It was fascinating, but the same time terrifying. Ember felt uncomfortable and shy, her head mindlessly playing tricks on her about the Prince choosing her on purpose. If Arlette concentrated hard enough, she could almost hear the Prince's voice in Ember's head, repeating the same words he'd told her the day she got severely mentally and physically unstable.

Arlette suddenly heard the oak doors open petrifyingly, along with the guardian's voice. "Let us all show reverence to our Highness," he paused, and Arlette bowed her head, sending quick prayers up the sky nervously.

Until now, Arlette hadn't realized that the King was sitting on the throne all this time. And she knew this because of his powerful presence coming from there. Only until now, until the Prince entered, she had notice it.

His familiarity washed over her, and it was stronger now, excruciatingly intense. She stayed with her head bow, of course, never moving. She took a small breath. Arlette could feel the girl beside her shake in anticipation, as if wanting to almost jump in place. Arlette wanted to slap her, kick some normal sense into her. But instead, she whispered, "I think you should calm down,"

The girl's only response was a scoff.

"Ladies? What did I say about not talking until you're allowed to?"

Arlette wanted to be swallowed whole by the ground. She didn't want to be the center of attention, she had enough experience with that already.

But the other girl took the blame, which surprised Arlette immensely. "I apologize, sir, it was my fault."

The guardian nor nobody else said anything.

"Let's begin, shall we?" The guardian started. "First, the Prince will regard you with some gestures. Such as looking in your eyes, taking your hand, etcetera, etcetera. The reason is because Fate usually shows those strong feelings through those simple actions…"

And just like that, everything started.

The Prince was left alone, and just like the guardian, he started from the far right. Arlette hadn't heard a word from him since he'd entered, which didn't really surprised her but taunt her.

Every time he went to the next girl, finding out that that wasn't the one, his presence came more strongly, stinging Arlette's mind. It was an endless torment for her.

And before Arlette knew it, the Prince was standing right in front of the girl before Arlette.

Nothing seemed to happen, so he moved on to Arlette.

And without warning, he took both of Arlette's hands in his. Arlette gasped in surprise. Not from the sudden gesture, but beneath it all. Beneath his rough, deprived hands, beneath feeling his spine-chilling existence, beneath everything else, she felt something deeper, more cavernous and obscure. Arlette had never experienced anything like this in her entire life. It was Fate, Fate was telling her something.

But the Prince let go of her hands, as if nothing had happened, as if he hadn't just felt the same complex intensity she did when they touched, and instead, went to the next girl.

Something deep inside Arlette silently sank, she pushed it away stubbornly though, deciding to drown in her own wonders and thoughts, not before someone let out an agonizing scream and soon, Arlette could hear heels desperately crackling away. The girl was sobbing loudly, pushing the oak door open. That girl was Ember.

One of the guardians shouted to follow her.

"Let her go, I know who she is," the Prince said calmly. "She's a bit... unstable,"

The girls started to whisper loudly to each other, gossiping what they had just witnessed.

"Ladies, quiet down please." The guardian instructed.

Tears prickled at the corners of Arlette's orbs, and she wished Ember was okay wherever she had run to. She sighed silently, hoping Cade was taking it more lightly. Hoping everything else would go lightly. As soon as this was over, Arlette will go to Ember. She had to go to Ember.

After everyone settled down, the guardian said, "The Prince has gone through all the girls. And we're all honored to ask him who was the lucky one Fate had chosen,"

Everyone waited, curiously anticipating for his answer.

"Her."

There was a dead silence.

Arlette could feel every single pair of eyes on her. She shook her head mentally. Maybe there was a misunderstanding. It could be the girl next to her for all she knew.

"Oh, our lovely number twenty..." there was a rustle of papers, "seven. Arlette."

Her face was drained from all blood she had left. Nobody seemed to notice her utter shock.

"Please stand beside him, miss, so all have the honor to meet the Prince's soon-to-be Princess." Arlette could sense the guardian's smile on his face.

And she couldn't believe this. Arlette's head was spinning, and she shook her head repeatedly, stepping back. "No, no, no, no, no," she whispered to herself, almost stumbling and falling back. One of the girls grabbed her hand, but she yanked it away.

She concentrated on where she last heard the oak door being open, and in an instant, grabbed her dress on either side, begging Fate for protection, and ran towards the exit, with no precise knowledge of where she was going. Arlette heard everyone yelling to go after her, but she kept running until she bumped against the hard wooden door. She quickly grazed for the handle, nervously pushing the big door open.

And she just... ran.

With no certain grasp of where she was going, she was swallowed into a long hallway, the strands of her hair falling out of her neat, combed hair style. And she realized that as soon as she'd stepped out of there, her heart felt some hollow, ardent, and distant longing. Like she'd left something she shouldn't have.

But she gradually pushed it away and kept running.

She could hear the guardians yelling in the distance, but she let the walls guide her. Arlette just hoped she was going on the right course. Maybe if she could find Ember, that would be much better...

Arlette was suddenly stopped full force, being dragged into a corner. She struggled to get away, trying to scream but couldn't since they were covering her mouth.

"Shut up, Arlette!" Ember whispered harshly against her ear as they both fell down. "It's me Ember," Arlette stopped struggling and tears quickly filled her eyes. Ember let go of her and Arlette hugged her. "Oh, Ember. I was so worried about you... Are you okay?"

They both stood back up.

"Yeah, I'm fine. I should be the one asking you that," Ember said apologetically. She paused and Arlette could hear her swallow. "I suppose he chose you...?" It was as if she was almost scared to say it. "Well, Fate did,"

Arlette nodded silently, her head bowed. "How do you know?"

"It isn't very hard when you hear thousands of guardians shouting to follow a girl, and I'd figured I know you a little too much to not know it was you."

Arlette chuckled silently, shaking her head at her sister.

"You should go back, Arlette." Arlette looked up, surprised. "It's too dangerous, you don't know what he's capable of."

Arlette couldn't believe her sister. "What?"

"Even if you don't go back to him, he'll find you, and that'll be worst." Her voice cracked. "Just go. Let the guardians find you." Ember turned Arlette around, pushing her lightly out towards the hallway.

"Ember...no. I'm not going anywhere near that... beast. We need to pack our things and run away. Far away from here." Arlette urged, taking Ember's hand in hers, while tears ran down her face.

Ember yanked her hand away. "No, Arlette. You are now bound to him. It doesn't matter where you go, he will always find you. Always." Ember took a breath, trying to calm herself, "Now go," she pushed Arlette out in the hallway.

Arlette turned around again. "Ember!"

But Ember was gone.

"There! Look! She's there. After her!" She heard one of the guardians instruct at the end of the hallway. Arlette ran the opposite direction, suddenly feeling strangely tired. She kept running, but tripped with her own dress, making her fall full force.

She tried to get up, but she couldn't, exhaustion was draining her whole. Arlette screamed in frustration as she clung against the walls. Her feet wobbled, and she fell down again. The dress was too heavy. Her head was too heavy. Everything was pondering, stinging, bothering. Arlette didn't want it to drag her. She didn't want to be dragged into darkness. She was light, not darkness. She had always been light.

But, now that she thought of it, she had always been darkness.

After all, that's all she saw.

Blind Beauty | 11

D edication goes to ILikeFarts for the beautiful banner on the side!

Chapter Once

Arlette's P.O.V.

Arlette was awake.

She turned lazily on her side, uncommonly feeling at complete peace. Her slumber had been heavy and seemingly long, but she was still tired, as if had carried a mountain over her shoulders. Arlette tried to ignore it though, and as she faced down on the soft, ample bed, she ran both her arms up and down, like a bird warming up its wings, feeling the soft and unfamiliar texture with her hands. Longing to stay here longer and sleep, she stopped.

Arlette turned and faced up and her heart panicked a little as it slowly started to hammer against her chest. Where was she? She sat up, pushing her hair out of her face. The room smelled of something vaguely familiar, but she couldn't quite put her finger on it. The room was deadly silent, and the only thing she could hear was her jumping heart. She slowly started to slide to the edge of the bed, her bare feet touching the cold, marble floor.

She flinched, not expecting it. But regardless, pressed both of them against the floor, standing up.

Dizziness instantly took over her, overwhelming her, and she trembled. Without minding the nausea, she gave a small step forward. After all, she needed to get out of here, she needed to escape. She gave another step, the feeling too overwhelming now. Her legs wobbled—they were tired and swollen.

She took deep breaths, trying to relax her tense muscles. Arlette tried to take another step, but not before she heard a voice that made her come to a bold halt, making her heart resonate through her ears.

"You never give up, do you?"

That's why it smells familiar in here. It smells like darkness—like him.

The voice came from somewhere in the same room, but Arlette could hear it everywhere, demonstrating that the bedroom was rather big.

"You need rest," he said, but Arlette was frozen in spot. She didn't move, she didn't breathe, she didn't do anything.

There was silence, but then—

"No," Arlette said through gritted teeth. She took another step. And another one, daring herself, and then another one, and then she started running, throwing away all the shuffling thoughts telling her to stay where she was, but before she could get remotely close to anything indicating the chance of escape, the Prince grabbed her roughly, and she screamed at the top of her lungs, crying for help.

He picked her up and threw her on the bed. Voices were screaming as he touched her, as if physical contact burned. She tried to get up, but the Prince was too strong, he held her down. Arlette felt him too close to her, and she kept on screaming, hoping somebody would be able to hear her and come to where they were. But nobody came and then she felt his lips on her ear as he whispered roughly, "Calm down or I'll make you sleep for weeks," his voice was threatening, dark, poisonous.

She stopped screaming.

Tears ran down her eyes as she started panting. She didn't like to show weakness, but she was just so worn out...

Never in her life had she felt so defeated and tired.

Arlette swallowed, trying to find her voice, "Just l-let me g-go,"

"No." He stepped away from her. "You're mine now. Fate chose you."

'Her.'

Arlette remembered pretty well, she just didn't want to accept it. So much had happened the past weeks, she didn't even know what to think.

I am no one's, she wanted to say, but stopped herself - for her own good.

"W-where am I?"

"My bedroom," he said matter-of-factly. "As if it wasn't obvious already by the paintings."

For some reason, Arlette felt a deep, abrupt pang in her chest. And it didn't even matter if he knew or not. There was a long silence before she replied, "I am blind, Your Highness."

Accidentally, Arlette didn't know why she wasn't putting on her mask—her flat, monotonous face. That face she gave everyone who she felt deserved it. That face where she looked at them straight where she heard their voices coming from, her head high, demanding respect. But, she instead bowed her head, as if for the first time, she was ashamed to her disability, something she had never felt until now.

The Prince didn't respond right away, he was silent.

"I-I…"

He didn't know what to say, so seconds later, he slammed the door behind him, making Arlette wince.

Dark lullabies hovered over her head, clouding her mind. Arlette grabbed a pillow, screaming into it. She then threw it to the side. Arlette was so frustrated and angry at herself, and she didn't even know why.

He must've been furious with her for not telling him. Arlette couldn't get off her mind the thought that he might punish her.

Arlette took deep breaths. Just stay calm.

But then a rather strange thought came into her mind.

He sleeps in this bed.

Arlette threw herself off the bed quickly, suddenly feeling embarrassed, but not before the door was being open.

"Dear, you need to go back to bed," she heard an elderly voice say, the door closing behind her.

Before she could've utter a word out, she felt the woman lacing her arms through hers, guiding her back to bed.

"But ma'am—"

"But ma'am nothing, child, you need to rest. Here, lay on the bed."

Forgetting the fact that she flew out of bed the moment she realized it was his, Arlette did as told, and soon enough, she could feel a hot, wet towel being placed on her forehead and her bare feet. Minutes later, she could feel her head stop pounding and her muscles loose a little.

The elderly woman did her work quietly.

"Drink this tea, dear, it'll relax your muscles." She leaned the cup against Arlette's lip, as she sat on the bed, the strong, hot scent surfing and invading her nostrils. Arlette took a small sip and the woman then lend her the cup. She took it gratefully, loving the taste of foreign herbs and the nice feeling of it.

Arlette felt so much better. "Thank you."

"It is no problem, miss," the woman said calmly, sincerely.

"Please call me Arlette,"

"Arlette..." she tasted the name, "such a beautiful name,"

"Thank you..." Arlette smiled. "What's your name?"

"Elsa,"

Arlette tried to taste her name on her lips too, "Elsa..." A little conversation wouldn't hurt, she guessed. "Why... are my muscles so tense and why do I feel so tired?"

"It's the stress. You've been too stressed and worried lately," she said thoughtfully. "But it's also something else," she said. "It's a force—his force. It's making you weak because you fight back. You never give in without a fight. Is that correct?"

Arlette nodded, simultaneously understanding.

"I suppose that was you who was screaming a while ago?"

She nodded again.

Elsa took both of Arlette's hands in hers, and Arlette could feel concern and a tint of fear coming off of her. "You need to stop fighting, Arlette. It's going to make you weak to the point where you won't be able to even stand up without passing out—"

"But Elsa, I—"

"I know you don't want this, but you can't live like this."

"Of course I can. If I could just escape—"

"He'll find you—he'll find you anywhere you go, Arlette, he's destined to be with you now. And Fate did that for a reason."

"But Fate knows—"

"Yes, Fate knew you didn't want this from the beginning. But it's the way things are, Arlette, and you have to accept them."

And this woman was correct, but something in Arlette always told her to push over her limits - to never fear, but try, the unknown. Maybe it was her consciousness, or maybe it was Fate—she didn't know. Because if she tried, if she pushed over her limits and not fear the unknown, she might get what she've been always looking for. Even though it will always put her in trouble or controversy. People always warned her to never grab for much, because at the end, you'll never grab enough.

But isn't that what we all want? To have anything we wish for? But as some people say: Be careful what you wish for, because you just might get it. But this doesn't exactly work for Arlette, does it?

Arlette sighed, her head vacant of any coherent answer, "I...I just want to see my family,"

Elsa stroked Arlette's hands. "When the right time comes you'll be able to. For now, just rest, dear, you need it." She placed one hand on Arlette's forehead after taking away the towel, and pressed a little, sending sleep to her brain. Before she was shoved all the way into her slumber, she heard Elsa whisper, "Be careful."

⊏

Arlette was nowhere and everywhere, she tried to differ between the two, but she couldn't. It was like she was in between, neither black or white. Grey perhaps. As she hightened her senses, she realized that there wasn't any type of smell whatsoever. Everything felt empty and out of place. There was no sound or emotion. Everything was just so... hollow.

"Oh dear, you've come back! Isn't this a lovely surprise..." It was her, the loud, evil woman she met in her last dream.

She tried looking for her by turning around. "Where am I?"

The woman sighed, irritated. "Honestly, honey, you need to get it together," she said. "You're the one who dreams of these places, not me."

"But I don't even think about them." Arlette gave several steps.

"Yet you would like to visit them, wouldn't you?" Arlette could feel the boastful smirk on her face.

She didn't answer, because in reality, it was true. She didn't know if she wanted to be in this place though, where she was unable to identify her surroundings. The woman continued, "How's it going with the beast?" But she didn't let Arlette form any type of answer. She laughed hysterically, as if what she was saying was some kind of inside joke. Arlette could feel her closer yet somehow still far away.

That sparked interest in Arlette. "You know him?"

"Oh yes I do, sweetheart," she contemplated, as if deep in some memories, and then she whispered in her ear, "Want me to tell you a secret?"

Arlette didn't even think about it. "No."

The woman laughed. "I'm going to tell you anyways," she said, then slowly murmured, "He was mine once." And then she let out another round of crazed laughter.

Arlette shook her head, stepping away. She wanted to go back—she wanted to awake. She didn't like this woman. Something was off with her—something was not right.

The woman stopped laughing. And then stood in front of Arlette, as her breath fanned her face, she whispered slowly, "But answer me this, dear. . . can a beast be tamed?"

"I...I don't know."

"But you will."

❑   ❑   ❑   ❑   ❑   ❑   ❑

Aaron's P.O.V.

"I heard that Fate chose her,"

"She did." He chuckled venously, running his thumb across his chin. "Funny how these news spread like wildfire."

Aaron didn't want to show how hurt he was by this unexpected news. He stayed a fair distance away from him. "You shouldn't have done what you did to her the other night." His fists clenched and unclenched in rage. He could feel beads of sweat roll down his forehead. And all he could hear was the screech of her agonizing screams.

Out of all the girls in the Fae lands, Fate chose her.

His heart sank.

Aaron couldn't face him the same night of the choosing. Something had happened and he was nowhere in sight. But now this was his opportunity to confront him.

"I didn't do anything," he said, his voice a deadly tone. Aaron looked at him, trying to read him, but there just was a tornado of thoughts and emotions. That infuriated him.

He came threateningly closer to his brother. "How dare you say that when you nearly exploded her brain?"

The trees around them rustled furiously, and the moon was starting to hide behind the clouds.

The Prince's pitch black pupils filled both of his eyes, showing his excru-ciating and perplexing rage. He talked slowly, with gritted teeth. "I did not do anything to her head." The veins on his neck and face looked like they were going to burst. They were turning a black-ish red, pumping disturbingly.

"Liar." And just like that, Aaron threw him a cold punch as hard as he could, hitting him square in the face.

The Prince stepped back, then snapped his head up as if nothing hap-pened, and snaking towards Aaron impossibly fast, he grabbed him by the neck, slamming him hard against a tree. Something cracked, and Aaron let out an agonizing scream. The Prince came close to his face. "You are no match for me, brother."

Aaron's breath was shallow as he felt like he was going to pass out from the outrageous pain in his whole back.

"You're not allowed to go near her," he inquired furiously as he gripped his neck stronger.

Aaron was losing himself. His head was spinning as he tried to find his voice, "S-she won't allow y-you to."

"I am not asking for her permission. You'll do as I say and that's it." With that said, he let go of him, and Aaron fell to the floor.

Grabbing his neck and coughing, he looked up at his brother, gazing at his grotesque and hideous self. "She will never be able to fall in love with someone as damaged as you. You're a monster."

The Prince looked at him. His face vacant of any emotion. He stayed quiet, his eyes burning into Aaron's. "Perhaps," he said, then Aaron's face flew painfully to the right, and blood started to accumulate inside his mouth.

Aaron's vision blurred and unfocused, everything around him was spinning comically. He shook his head, trying to make his eyes focus. It worked. And he couldn't feel the side of his face. It felt like it was ripped and shattered out of his face. He didn't dare touch it.

When Aaron looked back up, the Prince was gone.

Spitting the blood from the cold punch his brother gave him, he weakly stood up, wobbling his way back to the palace.

He only wished he could see Arlette one last time.

Blind Beauty | 12

A /n: All I can say is that this chapter was an utter ass to write. I love it and hate it. Dedicated to palenomian101 for the amazing drawing of the Beast! I never expected anything like this so thank you so much, I really, really love it. Thank you.

THIS WILL BE EDITED.

Chapter Doce

"Arlette," a voice urged, shaking her rather madly.

Arlette groaned, turning away.

"Wake up," it hissed.

She thought she didn't recognize the voice but then—

"Ember?" Arlette frowned, feeling confused as she slowly started to turn and place herself in a sitting position.

Ember sounded relieved. "Yes, yes, that's me. I was afraid you won't be able to recognize me."

Arlette felt a bit light headed, but she didn't pay attention to it. "Why wouldn't I?" She mumbled, half asleep.

Ember thought about it. "I don't know, really. I'm just really worried. I haven't seen you since the day of the choosing."

Arlette frowned, shifting slowly in place. "Was that so long ago?" She had lost track of time—of everything, really.

"A little bit over a week."

Arlette's eyes widened in shock. "What?" Was she asleep this whole time?

Where has the Prince been sleeping then?

Most certainly not with her.

"Mom, dad, and grandma had been worried sick about you." Ember said, taking Arlette's hands in hers, she was talking fast, as if she was in a hurry. "And I just needed to see you to make sure you were alright." Arlette sensed fear and desperation.

Arlette tried to remember everything that happened that night. She remembered it all. And it felt like it had just happened.

Something came to her mind.

"But where were mom, dad, and grandma? I didn't sense them..." She trailed off, confused.

"They were somewhere. We couldn't see them, but they could. We were behind some invisible shield or something..." Ember said thoughtfully.

Arlette was quite surprised as she nodded. She sensed that if she asked Ember how'd she knew, Ember wouldn't tell her, so she stayed quiet.

"How'd you get in here?" Arlette then asked, curious.

"It doesn't matter. I gotta go now," she hugged Arlette briefly, "someone's coming." Ember said quickly, letting go of Arlette.

Arlette quickly stopped her by grabbing her hand before she could go any further. It pained her that her sister had to go just like that. "Wait, Ember..." Tears pricked at the corners of her green orbs. "Tell them I'll see them soon."

Ember was silent before she found her voice. "I will,"

Ember made a move to go, but Arlette held her hand tighter, "Are you going to be okay?"

"Yeah, don't worry about me, I'll be fine. I promise."

Arlette nodded, mentally trying to convince herself.

And then she let her hand go. Seconds later, she could hear something click open. It wasn't the bedroom door. It was a window, maybe a balcony door. A soft breeze made its way towards Arlette, blowing her dress. Arlette frowned briefly, skimming her hands over the unfamiliar dress.

The door closed quietly back again, and Arlette felt her stomach twist and clung in itself. She didn't dare turned towards it though. And as she ran her hands over her face, she hadn't realized she was crying, and all she really wanted to do was scream until she no longer had the strenght to. She wanted for the emptiness to swallow her and wrap itself around her. She wanted to dream. To go somewhere—someplace not real.

She heard the door creak open.

Arlette didn't move, didn't flinch, didn't blink, didn't do anything.

She just... stood there.

"Miss, are you okay?" A feminine voice asked as the door closed behind her.

Arlette's head snapped up towards the voice. She cleared her throat, quickly wiping away her tears. "Y-yeah, I'm fine."

"The Prince ordered for you to eat lunch. I have it here."

This was stupid.

"And why can't I have it down there with my family?"

The girl hesitated. "He doesn't quite trust you, miss."

Arlette sighed, irritated. "I'm not hungry," she lied.

She felt the girl approach her, chuckling as she said, "Oh, believe me, miss, you are. You haven't eaten in a lil' over a week. That is enough for anyone to be starvin'."

"But—"

"Please," she pressed. "The Prince wouldn't like to see this plate untouched."

The thought to make him angry was rather tempting, something in Arlette always expected for more even though every time he was angry, the fear and terror that crept inside her veins was unbearable. Arlette mentally slapped herself, disappointed at her stupid swirling thoughts.

The girl walked pass Arlette. "I'll leave it here on the bed and when I come back, I want to see it clean!" She joked. Arlette chuckled. Her voice was funny.

The strange girl laughed too, saying, "If you need anythin' else, do not hesitate to call me, I'll be right down the hallway." She started to walk away towards the door.

"Wait!" Arlette said, following her footsteps.

"Yes, miss?"

"Would you mind if I ask you to stay here—with me?"

The girl hesitated. "But, miss, I'm merely a maid—"

"It doesn't matter," Arlette smiled. She was tired of being alone and making a friend seemed convenient right now. "I just want some company,"

"Okay," the girl said enthusiastically, it seemed like she almost couldn't contain herself, she was going to burst.

Arlette laughed. "What's your name?"

"Daisy," the girl said almost proudly, and Arlette nodded, smiling.

"What's your name, miss?"

"Arlette,"

"Such a pretty name," Daisy contemplated. "You must be really excited for next week." She said excitedly.

Arlette frowned at that. "What's happening next week?"

"The Grand Ball is happening!" She chirped, suddenly taking both of Arlette's hands. "Since there hasn't been any female livin' in the palace for almost a century—because the King's wife died almost a century ago—there hasn't been any Grand Ball, but since you're here, there's finally one!" She twirled with Arlette in a dancing motion, both of their arms extended as they went round and round.

Arlette frowned in the mists of the Daisy's madness. "Who's going to be there?"

"Everybody!" She boomed, twirling around and around with Arlette. "All the Princes and Kings and Princesses and villagers from the other sides!" She sang, swinging Arlette back and forth.

Arlette thought about this.

"And why are you so excited?" Arlette asked her, confused like no other.

Daisy came to halt, letting go of Arlette. Arlette was startled by the sudden halt. All the twirling around left her dizzy.

"Why?" She asked, more calmed now. "Because, we maids, get to make your dress out of the best materials. Our hands are gifted by the very Fate," she remarked. "And because is one of most important events in all history; the Prince is going to show you off."

Fate loved Arlette. She really did. Everything opposite of what she wanted was happening. So she might as well put it that way; Fate loved Arlette.

Arlette ran a hand through her tangled hair, sighing.

"Oh, but don't worry. Everything is gonna be fine."

Yeah, because you're not the one trying to run away from him.

Arlette tried changed the subject. These news where too much. "Can you guide me to where the bathroom is? I think I need a bath…"

"Sure." Daisy said, lacing her arm through Arlette's and walking up east. They didn't walk out of the room, so that meant that she was going to take a bath in his bathroom.

Lovely.

"I brought clothes and a comb just in case. They're on the bed." Daisy said as Arlette stepped inside the bathroom and grabbed the towel that Daisy was handing her.

Arlette nodded wordlessly, grabbing the handler and closing the door.

She then leaned her back against it.

Can anything just get any worst?

Arlette didn't know what she was going to do now. She couldn't run away—he'd find her. She couldn't do anything really, because he'd find her. Stupid, she thought, how she got "caught" when all along what she'd been doing was run away. Run away from Fate, basically. And from her destiny—from her future. Arlette couldn't believe she was giving up. Regardless, she had to. Lonely tears ran down her face as the familiar sad, hollow voices sang silently in her ear. Something inside her head was telling her something from this upheaval and crazy situation was coming out though. Something good. Maybe not now, but it was. She was hopeful. She won't escape or fight back. She will do what Fate wants her to do.

Arlette stepped into the tub with her mind set.

Or maybe not.

Beast's P.O.V.

He didn't know if he should stay here or go and apologize for his atrocious behavior. It was foolish to say such thing. But all along, he hadn't noticed. How hadn't he? He wondered. He was so perplexed with all of her being that he had not noticed such a small, but definitely certain thing.

He paced around the living room with restlessness settled heavily upon him. He wanted to get his mind off of her, he wanted to get out of this place, and he had done it, but he had done everything he had to this this morning - just to get his mind off of her.

At last, he decided to go.

He had been sleeping in one of the other rooms for his own sake, or maybe hers, which has been as stressing as letting her sleep in his.

Without realizing it, he'd been in front of his room door, where, on the other side, her heavenly body might be sleeping or doing something she shouldn't.

He hesitated, before deciding to knock.

A few seconds later, he waited but she didn't answer nor open the door.

Thinking she might be asleep, he grabbed the big door's handle, clicking it open.

His room smelled heavily of her. Her alluring scent was everywhere. The beast breathed in heavily, enjoying how it felt to do it. But as he was doing so, something inside him thrashed and screamed - something as close as a furious...craving. He pushed it away roughly as he closed the door behind him. His eyes falling on the bed, which was empty and neatly made. Her food laid on the drawer untouched, cold. He quickly wondered where she was. But soon, as silence strained in, he could hear an soft humming coming from the bathroom - it was beautiful, foreign. But almost instantly, it stopped. He glanced at the bathroom door attentively, then at the balcony. She couldn't possibly made a escape, could she? But what about the humming coming from bathroom?

As if on cue, the bathroom's door opened. His head snapped toward it, and she gasped.

And there she stood. She was just so beautiful. The most beautiful creature he has ever seen. Green, twinkly orbs hiding secrets, pink lips slightly plumped and small, beautiful body covered away from others' forbidden thoughts. Small droplets of water ran slowing down her temple and neck as she stood there rather frozen.

He swore he could stare at her forever.

Suddenly, she quickly walked past him, standing on the other side of the room. His eyes followed her quietly. She bowed her head slowly, her arms wrapped tightly around herself as her cheeks reddened. "If you don't mind, your Highness, I need some privacy."

Her voice was so angelic, so innocent. It was feverishly hard to control himself. He swallowed, something he barely even do, and cleared his throat.

"I came to apologize. I should have never been so..." he tried to find the best word, "cruel." Kind of ironic, he thought. But he didn't pay much attention to it. "Please, forgive me." He walked toward her slowly, and she backed away.

"I don't think this is the best moment to do that, your Highness. Right now, I need privacy." He voice was monotonous, along with her face.

He came even closer to her, and he heard her bump her back against the wall behind her as he backed away. It was amazing how he made not even the slightest sound and she could still know, or perhaps feel, that he was coming toward her.

She was trapped between the wall and him now. Her breathing was hard, rapid. He could hear her heart thumping against her chest vigorously. Her scent was warmly wrapping itself around him slowly as the seconds ticked, and his veins bumped madly as he tried to control himself.

It had never been this difficult.

He lowered his head down to her ear slowly. "Why must you always fight back?" He whispered, feeling as he talked like he normally would, she would escape, or worse, disappear. Fate has brought her to him for a reason. And time was ticking.

"It is a need," she said quietly.

"Or else?"

She hesitated before answering.

"Or else I feel useless."

Right after she said it, it looked like she'd just realized she'd said something forbidden. "I-I..."

He grabbed her chin, gently pushing her face up. Her eyes were filled with tears.

He didn't think much about it - he kissed her.

She gasped, but surprisingly, didn't turn away.

He wondered why.

It was slow at first. But then he couldn't control himself - his burning, savage hunger took over him, making him wrap his strong arms around her, deepening the kiss. She instantly responded, her small, soothing hand on his cheek, as her soft lips ran ardently over his. Hearts thumped rapidly as blood of passion boiled. He pushed her bare leg up around his hip, pressing himself against her.

She gasped, arching her back.

He went down to her cool neck, pressing hot, passionate kisses along it. She grabbed the back of his head softly, breathing in heavily.

Her touch was an electrifying, potent, and beautiful feel.

Everything was a fiery bliss, yet still so hotly real. Never in his entire, long life had he ever felt this way. Not even with Simone. This was stronger, more powerful, more deeper.

But then her towel fell.

She instantly pushed him away from her, reality sinking, quickly grabbing the towel and wrapping it back protectively around herself.

He stopped himself from seeing anything he shouldn't.

Her body rested against the wall as she breathed heavily, finding her lost breath. Her face was flushed. She didn't say anything and neither did he. The only thing that could be heard was their panting and feel the hot, ardent air hovering around them.

The smell of her was stronger, indicating her hidden heat. It called to him, telling him that this wasn't over yet, but he restrained himself from doing something he'd probably regret... and just like that, he left the room.

Blind Beauty | 13

A /n: Not the best chapter but I think you'll like I apologize for taking so long guys, I was just too busy to write. Also, sorry in advance if there are any mistakes. I'll fix them later.

Chapter Trece

Arlette combed her hair silently, running the comb smoothly over her damp hair. She didn't know how she felt. There was an odd, mixture of distant feelings. They were calling to her, trying to make her remember what happened just moments ago. But she didn't want to, even though she still felt her heart thumped madly against her chest, reminding her every second of it. It didn't quite bother her the fact that the Beast was her first kiss, and she didn't know if it should, but it was how he made her feel.

Perhaps he was too blind behind his ravishing desire to notice, but the way he made her feel was so enthralling, consuming, so captivatingly deadly... Arlette felt as if she was going to explode, or worse, disappear. She didn't even know she could feel that way. So many strong feelings - so many thoughts. They consumed her, lost her, and reappeared back again when she went back to reality. They were so difficult to be able to explain, even to herself. Arlette wondered if he felt the same, or even a string of it.

She put the comb on the drawer, standing up and running her hands over it, hoping for her cane. She hasn't use it for what felt like ages. Not finding it, she sighed, running her hands accustomedly down her dress until she felt something in her pocket. Her cane. Arlette pulled it out, quickly snatching it open.

Maybe it was instinct.

Arlette started walking. This wouldn't hurt, she guessed, extending her arm and grabbing the door's handle, she clicked it open. Cautiously opening the door, she slided out, closing it silently behind her. Arlette promised herself that she wouldn't try to escape, it was pointless anyways. She just wanted out.

Carefully walking down the long hallway, everything was deadly silent. The only thing that she could hear was her own muffled footsteps against the carpeted floor. Arlette didn't know if that was a good or bad thing—the hallway being so quiet that is. The hallway was endlessly long, as always. She made a couple of turns. And as Arlette kept walking she heard distant laughter. Stopping abruptly, she wondered if she should go back to the room.

Maybe she should go back, but of course, she didn't want to. Curiosity always got the best of her.

Cornering herself to the left, walking slowly as she hear inaudible voices become clear, Arlette stopped, placing the cane in her dress pocket.

It was feminine—the voice. But she didn't recognize it.

"Don't you sometimes wonder why the Prince's chosen one never comes out of the palace? I mean, I've never seen her before. I've only heard the rumors of her unmistakable beauty."

Arlette frowned.

"That's none of our business, Val, just keep folding the blankets." Said the other girl nonchalantly.

"They say her hair looks powerful. It's as red as fire," she dragged the word, surprised even as she said it, "red, Marr. She was born with red hair. Do you know what my grandma told me about girls that are born with red hair?"

Arlette wanted to hear this. Her hair was always a big deal to everyone else. No one dared tell her about it though. Not even her family. When she was younger, she would ask her mother and grandma about it, but they always avoided the subject. Seeing that she wouldn't get a response, she reluctantly stopped asking.

"She told me—"

"Val!" The other girl hissed. "Stop talking about her. You know we can't talk about anyone who lives in the palace."

"Yet we still do."

"You do. I stopped after the last time we got caught."

Arlette suddenly heard distant footsteps coming from the hallway.

She didn't have another option, they were going to see her anyway - one way or the other.

The girls were still arguing over whose fault was it.

Walking out of her hidden place, not two full seconds passed and the girls' voices came to a halt as Arlette felt their eyes falling intensely on her.

"Miss…" Both of them breathed in unison, and Arlette quickly felt some kind of reverence towards her. Were they bowing? "Good evening."

She had stopped briefly, facing toward them. She bowed too. Sensing their nervousness, she smiled at them a little, replying, "Good evening."

Arlette wondered if that was a nice greeting. She wasn't really what you would call social. But she tried.

But she wasn't about to make conversation, she made it precisely to another door as she kept walking, opening and sliding in, or out, who knew?

Much to her displeasure, it was another room, much more spacious and ample - maybe a living room.

She rested her back against the door, thinking about using her cane but deciding against it. Arlette wanted to figure out this place. She was staying here, or at least that's what she thought.

"Arlette?" Someone asked surprised as if not believing their eyes.

Her head snapped towards the voice.

"What are you doing here?"

"Aaron?" She followed the voice, her steps long and quick, seconds later, being crashed in a warming embrace.

"Arlette..." he breathed, sounding relieved. Aaron buried his face against her neck, breathing her in. She returned the embrace, hugging him tightly. He groaned a little at the gesture, but didn't pull away.

She did though.

"What's wrong?" She frowned. That was from pain, Arlette felt it.

"Nothing's wrong. Don't worry about it, Arlette." He said, hugging her again. "I thought I'd never see you again."

But she wasn't having it. Arlette pulled away once again. "Aaron, you're hurt."

He sighed. "That was a while ago, I'm healing now."

"Is it your back?"

Arlette took his silence as confirmation.

"Who did this to you?" She wondered why someone would want to hurt Aaron. He was the King's son. You wouldn't exactly see this every day.

He didn't answer. But Arlette had a pretty good idea of who it was.

Arlette thought hard about it.

"Take off your shirt." Arlette said, rather determined. Her mother wasn't here to tell her not to do what she was about to do again.

Aaron didn't protest, and Arlette heard as he slowly took his several layers of upper clothes.

"Turn around," she instructed.

Arlette could feel him hesitate.

"Aaron..."

Aaron sighed, finally turning around.

"Relax and breathe," she whispered, concentrating as she slowly pressed her hand right in the middle of his spine.

Aaron groaned softly.

"Relax..." Arlette advised, pressing her hand a little bit deeper. She could feel him breathe heavily. And Arlette started to pull forces from the above, hoping for what she was looking for.

Arlette then ran both of her hands over his back, breathing in heavily, and all at once, pulled them away. She stepped away, feeling Aaron's eyes on her as he turned around. It had been a long time since she last did that. It felt good. She felt her senses stimulated, even more than they already were, and she felt hot inside. Like she could burst. It felt scary, as if she was holding too much of something.

Last time she had done this to someone, her mother was furious. Arlette couldn't understand. She was only six at the time. She was just trying to help.

"I only numbed the pain. But the damage is still there. You should see a healer, Aaron." Arlette said distantly, lost in the memory of the first and last time she did that. Only now had she tried it again, but with Aaron.

It was a hot, summer day. Arlette remembered as she sang, running around outside in the meadow, that it was rather too hot. She was playing under a big, oak tree though, which was fine with her. But she worried for Ember. She usually fell asleep in the small balcony, where the sun hit full force.

Running inside, she made her way carefully to the balcony, making sure that Ember wasn't there. Her mother was washing the clothes, grandma had been sleeping, and her dad was working.

Arlette approached the balcony hesitantly, stopping when she felt her little feet touch something. She crouched down, running her hands over a familiar body.

Ember.

Her clothes were hot as Arlette ran her hands over them, Ember was facing up, laying completely still. Arlette touched her face. It was burning hot and the skin was almost peeled off.

If she told her mom she wouldn't let them play outside. And that was Arlette's favorite thing to do.

Arlette shook her shoulders, frustrated, but at the same time worried because her face was literally frying.

Ember groaned, whinnying in pain as Arlette touched her face.

"I told you not to eat those flowers, Ember! They have dreamy dust."

Someone could be stabbing you, but if you were asleep under dreamy dust, you wouldn't feel a thing.

Now it had worn off Ember.

To be an eight year old at the time, Ember sure acted younger.

"My face..." Ember started sobbing. "It hurts, Arlette."

"But we can't tell mommy!" Arlette protested in her little six year old voice.

"Please..." Arlette sensed desperation and pain. "Do something then."

Arlette helped her sister up, and they went to a corner inside the cottage.

Tears started coming out of Arlette's little orbs, "What are we going to do, Ember?"

"Concentrate, Arlette." She pressed. "Don't think about anything else. Just taking away the pain."

"But we need medicine like the healers."

"Healers take a long time with their herbs. Come on, Arlette." Ember took Arlette's small hand, placing over her hot cheek hesitantly.

"Concentrate..." Ember whispered.

Arlette did as told. She concentrated, shoving away all thoughts and placing her mind on nothing else but taking away her sister's pain.

Moments later, she felt like she was pulling some kind of force, she was breathing it in, letting it slide inside her veins and vigiriously run down her palm. Letting out a long breath, she pulled her small hand away.

"You did it!" Ember hugged her, then ran outside, calling her mother. Arlette ran outside too, following her sister.

"Mom! Mom! Arlette fixed me!"

"What?" her mother ask, as if she didn't hear Ember clearly.

"Look!"

Her mother was silent for a moment. "Oh my... Where's Arlette?"

"She's right here behind me."

Arlette felt her sister move to the side, and as soon as she did, she heard her mom let out a morbid gasp.

"Arlette..."

She snapped out of the memory at Aaron's breathless, surprised voice.

"What?" Arlette asked confused, feeling like her voice was too loud for her own ears.

"Your—your...hair..."

Arlette touched her hair, frowning. But it felt normal, she didn't feel anything on it either.

"It's glowing..." He mused breathless. "Like it's... going to burst on fire."

He came closer to her. Arlette was starting to get scared.

"And your eyes..." he said. "They're completely clouded."

Blind Beauty | 14

Chapter Catorce

The air around Arlette was heavy and uncomfortable, like there was tension, but there really wasn't. And it suddenly smelled of roses and smooth grass, one of the many things that she missed from nature. Arlette was questioning her senses and feels—they were all over the place, like she couldn't control them, and she really couldn't... or was it just a side effect to how she was feeling? Or was it both? She didn't know. And as Arlette opened her mouth to say something anything—anything to question what Aaron was really seeing, the sound drained at the slamming of a door behind her and poisoning darkness rapidly lurking in. It slapped Arlette, making shivers bitterly swim over her spine. The nice smell quickly faded away.

Oh no.

Everything just happened so fast.

Arlette wished she could just disappear.

"I told you not to go near her," He was so angry, the flaming, vicious rage pouring off of him was sickening. The familiarity of his great darkness poured all over her, like pounding, hard rain. But then it felt like it was stroking her skin and senses and mind. It was overwhelming and feverish.

Arlette felt a rush of wind beside her, heard a deep groan coming from Aaron, then a hard slamming against one of the walls. He cried out in pure, blunt pain. The sound penetrated through the whole room, shaking the strong walls.

Arlette fell to her knees at the sudden pain shooting deep inside her back. She screamed at the top of her lungs. And as she quickly felt, and heard, the bones cracking painfully, she let out another agonizing scream, feeling her back shattering into pieces. The excruciating, ruthless pain she felt spreaded through her whole body, making her shudder and tremble. Her nostrils filled with the pure stench of death as if there was a rotting body right under her nose.

As she struggled, Arlette only knew one thing at the moment.

She had let out the same savage scream that Aaron had, probably worse, which could only mean one thing.

And it would not end well.

Everything then went frighteningly silent.

Arlette could feel her back bones achingly sticking out—never out of the skin though. Not being able to move a single muscle, she could feel them as if they were thick thorns coming from out of her own body, like she just suddenly grew them, but they hurt. The pain was blunt and gore. She felt like she could just die at any moment. As she breathed, they painfully bothered her insides and her chest, making her breathing shallow and ragged, forced also. Arlette hunched her back, trying to ease the pain, but ended up screaming horribly at her own move.

Arlette only knew one certain, very clear thing.

Her back was shattered. Badly.

"Oh Lord...look at her back." Aaron said quietly, completely astonished. It was like he, or they, were afraid to go near her, for the Prince did not do nor said anything either. It was like everything and everyone were frozen in spot. Arlette didn't sense a muscle move, even in her battered state.

But instantly, Arlette knew that Aaron was not saying that because of the disturbing, nauseating view of her back, but the fact that it was miraculously healing.

□   □   □   □   □   □   □

Aaron's P.O.V.

Aaron didn't mind the twisting, corrupted pain in his whole back, or at least he tried to push it away, or the fact that his brother was holding him up against a wall about to strangle him and rip his throat apart, who was also glancing back at her, but he could only stare in utter wonder and awe as Arlette's back healed with atrocity.

Arlette was on her knees, gasping rather loudly as the bones cracked slowly back into place, the skin beneath the dress moved abnormally, the bones sticking loudly to one another. The sound was morbid, yet stunning. Arlette let out a ear splitting scream, arching her back—the sound sorrowful, miserable. The view itself was wickedly amusing to watch. He had never seen anything like this before.

The Beast suddenly let go of Aaron, letting him fall with a hard thud on the floor. Aaron groaned, but quickly looked up at his brother, waiting for him to finish what he had started. But instead, the Prince turned around toward Arlette, who was trembling in fear, perhaps at what she had just witnessed.

Aaron looked at her back.

It was like new.

Glancing at his brother, Aaron saw as the Prince, as always highly and neatly dressed, showing great royalty and power, stared at her from the far distance where they were. The Prince knew he couldn't go near her if he didn't want to hurt her. His rage was a reckless and highly dangerous thing right now. It had always been. But right at this moment, it wasn't exactly as pretty. And even though Aaron didn't know much about his brother, despite the years growing together, he did know this.

And though he looked more calm now, Aaron noticed that he wasn't risking it.

He cares for her.

That only, somehow, triggered a wild emotion deep inside Aaron.

"Why is her hair—"

"Glowing? Like it's about to burst in a million flames?" Aaron inquired from behind, though looking at Arlette as well. He thought perhaps he was the only one seeing what he was seeing, but his brother just proved him wrong. He didn't know why he thought his eyes were deceiving him, but he had never seen such thing.

Aaron was waiting for his brother to also talk about her eyes, but she was looking down, trembling uncontrollably. And not until now, he couldn't understand why he had the old pain of his back, the one where he was healing slowly, the one in which Arlette had tried, and succeeded, to numb, and not the one he felt he had received from his brother, which Arlette felt as well.

Only one thing didn't happen.

His back didn't completely crack like Arlette's. Or at least that is what he felt.

"My mother..." Arlette whispered, disturbing Aaron's thoughts. "Take me to my mother."

As soon as those words escaped her lips, the Beast didn't hesitate. He picked her up from the floor effortlessly, and took her out of the room at the blink of an eye.

☐   ☐   ☐   ☐   ☐   ☐   ☐

Arlette's P.O.V.

Arlette gasped at the Prince's sudden action. They were moving very fast. It felt as if the Prince was running, but he wasn't. Just before she could say anything, he promised, "I won't hurt you."

It sounded convincing, sincere, and as much as she tried not to believe him, Arlette deep down knew that he was telling the truth.

She stayed quiet—they both did.

The Prince was warm and strong. Arlette felt a sense of safety despite the voices in her head screeching and thrashing. Pretty soon, she felt how the voices of the past were pulling her back into the memory that Aaron had disturbed. It was scary, but then again, why back down now when you were too deep in it?

"Arlette, never in your life do that again! That's bad, bad, bad! Good girls don't do that!" Yelled her mother furiously once they were inside.

Her mother had practically shoved her inside, sitting her roughly on a chair. Tears started running down Arlette's little face as she tried to explain, "M-mommy, I-I-I was trying to h-help Ember, I didn't know. I-I promise—"

"Quiet, Arlette," hushed her mother exasperated with Arlette's babbling, she wasn't listening to any of it. Her mother started pacing back and forth whispering to herself —she didn't know what to do.

"What's all this?" Questioned her grandma in a sonorous voice.

All the commotion had awaken her.

"Mother, look at her," inquired her mother miserably, defeatingly. "Can you explain why she did that now? In such a young age? Can you explain to me why she looks so different? In my knowledge, that wasn't suppose to happen!"

Her mother was nearly losing it as her grandma stayed silent. As seconds ticked by, Arlette felt her grandma slowly approach her.

She crouched down Arlette's level, grabbing her chin gently. "Oh dear..." whispered her grandma, pushing a strand of her hair behind her ear. Arlette could feel a vague fear and consternation blurrily coming from her grandmother.

"Lena, bring me the orchid wind." Arlette's grandma instructed to her mother. "It'll fade away the silver of her eyes."

Arlette quickly heard her mother rushing into one of the cottage's rooms, her steps fading quickly.

"Grandma...what's happening?" Ember asked, her voice flattering.

She was going to answer but a chirpy, loud voice interrupted her.

"Grandma! Look what I found!"

"Cade? Where have you been, child?" Asked grandma in confusion.

"I was playing with Nedi," Cade said simply.

She sighed. But kept quiet.

Arlette was silent the whole time. She felt like she should talk, but what would she say? There was nothing to say.

"Is it this?" Asked Lena as Arlette felt her come near her grandma.

"Yes. Give it to me."

Arlette heard something being softly popped open. The smell was a soft, feathery smell.

"Keep your head steady, Arlette, and your eyes open."

Arlette was starting to get scared. "Grandma—"

"Do it, dear," interrupted her grandma. "You'll be okay."

As Arlette nodded, she felt as her grandma blew the scented, strange wind-like substance against her eyes. She could feel as the warm wind wrapped around them making her feel odd. She blinked and it was gone.

"What about her hair?" Asked Lena, sounding exasperated.

"Only time will fix that." Her grandma answered. "But Lena, we need to talk about this."

"Arlette!"

It was her mother.

Arlette jumped, startled. She was still being carried.

In someone else's arms though.

A guardian's.

"What have you done, dear..." Arlette heard her mother say quietly as she heard footsteps come cautiously toward her.

Where was the Prince?

The guardian placed her on her feet gently, and she could feel him step back. Arlette turned around and bowed a thanks. She could soon feel the guardian bow too, stepping quietly out of the room.

Arlette's mother was coming toward her, but Arlette stepped back stubbornly. Her mother stopped and sighed.

"Mom..." Arlette said slowly. "What is happening to me?"

But she ignored Arlette's question. "You shouldn't have done that. You don't know what you're provoking against all of us."

Provoking, there's that word again, Arlette thought. Her mother had always used that word when Arlette did something that angered her. In this instance, it was certain she wouldn't have miss it. Arlette threw her arms up in the air, not believing her mother. Why did she always got to talk in codes? "I don't know what you're talking about, mom!"

"You should never had done that, Arlette! Not ten years ago nor now! You should've listened to your grandma when she told you not to do that." Her mother said angrily, breathing deeply.

"Maybe if you explained to me perhaps I would know what I'm getting myself into by the term you've always used—'provoking'!"

"Oh Arlette! There are things that are meant to remain secrets, we can't just spread them out like wildfire."

"You don't have to, you just had to warn me, not everybody else." Arlette crossed her arms across her chest, anger blooming immensely from inside her.

"I did! We all did, Arlette. Eric, me, your grandma, even Ember and Cade, but you never listen! You just follow what your heart and mind tell you to do, but sometimes you have to be aware of the consequences. Your heart is not always your best companion, neither is your mind."

And there was her mother again, talking her Fae talk.

Arlette opened her mouth to say something, but she heard a door open, accompanied by multiple voices.

Her head snapped toward them.

"Arlette?" her grandma asked, as if not believing her eyes. "Oh Lord..."

Arlette soon was crushed in a warm, bear hug from her grandmother. She relaxed and hugged her back, glad she was here.

"I told you I heard her," said Ember satisfied. "Arlette is too loud when she's angry."

If the situation wasn't as tense Arlette would've probably laugh at her sister.

"Oh my..." mused Cade, probably because of Arlette's noticeable alterations.

"She did it again, mother, she did it again," said Arlette's mother matter-of-factly.

"I can see that." Her grandma said, pulling away. Grabbing Arlette chin, she asked, "On who?"

Arlette frowned.

"Aaron," said Arlette carefully.

Ember and Cade gasped.

"She's not even old enough, mother!" Burst her mother frustratingly.

"Quiet, Lena." Hushed her grandma, sighing. "You haven't seen your daughter for over a week and this is how you greet her?" She sighed again. "She didn't do it fully. If she did, believe me, Lena, she wouldn't be this...tamed."

---

a/n: UNEDITED. I'm so sorry for the delay guys, chapters are getting kind of difficult to write, to be honest. But things are getting serious, aren't they? o.o Comment your thoughts! I'd love to see what you get to think of this chapter...Vote also! I would love you 5ever <3

p.s Banner is coming soon. I was too eager to wait, lol.

- nessie xoxo

Blind Beauty | 15

B eautiful banner on the side by severuslexus!

Chapter Quince

Arlette was uncomfortable. She had completely forgotten how bad and awful were the side effects of the orchid wind, which was the substance her grandma had blown once again against her eyes. Strangely enough, it made her sweat all over and have something remotely close to palpitations. Her eyes got watery from time to time and she felt upset without any convenient reason. Her grandma had told her that the orchid wind was supposed to fadely, vaguely, tame her. Arlette felt she could laugh at her words; for Arlette never considered herself to be someone as reckless and wild to the point of using something scarcely helpful and essential. The words leaving her grandma's lips sounded foreign and strange for some reason.

And here was the thing:

There was always something to treat something. Nothing was ever left out. Arlette could say she was amazed at how many medicines and herbs and spells and weird stuff there was to treat odd, almost-non-existent illnesses, which often never really worked—only by a slight chance, or if the healer was a very experienced one.

But, right now, she only knew one thing and one thing only:

Arlette hated these stupid methods.

And she was sweating, something close to crying, and ultimately upset.

"Can someone now explain to me what's happening?" Arlette was exasperated. She cracked her neck uncomfortably. "I," she pointed to herself, the side effects were really getting at her, "Arlette, supposedly healed my own, completely deteriorated back and there was no magic spell or anything! Ha! How wonderful is that? Is there anything else I'm able to do?" Her voice was mocking as she walked passed her grandmother, stretching her arms on either side and looking up towards the sky, saying, "Like fly?"

Her head spun dizzily at the action. And Ember giggled.

"Arlette, don't be a fool," her grandma said disappointedly.

"Don't be a fool?" Arlette asked incredulously, retreating her arms, and walking back toward her grandma. She felt her mother grab her, but she yanked her arm right away. "I'm the one who's going through this odd...phase, I'm the one who's spine shattered and healed in less than a whole minute, I'm the one feeling funny, I'm the one to be last of knowing anything when it comes to this family! And you're telling me not to be a fool?" Arlette couldn't believe her grandma right now.

"Arlette! Don't talk to your grandmother like that!" Her mother yelled, grabbing her arm forcefully and turning Arlette to face her mother. "The tongue is one of the worst enemies, we need to know how to use it," she hissed.

"Leave her, Lena. It's true and you know it."

Arlette had known and was conscious of the fact that she had disrespected her grandmother to a certain level and that she was acting like a totally spoiled, rotten girl, or maybe it was the side effects, like mentioned before, but above all, Arlette just wanted to be understood—at least that's what she thought. Her mother let go of Arlette, leaving her arm slightly throbbing from the dead grip. Arlette didn't mind.

Her mother walked off to what could be a corner.

"Arlette, we need to talk," inquired her grandma calmy, and Arlette could feel her soft scent walk passed her. She heard her grandma as she sat down.

Arlette felt herself flutter calm a little despite how uncomfortable she felt. But one way or the other, she had to. There were things to be said and explained. Arlette was confused, baffled, terrified of what happened—or whatever was happening to her in general, and besides, she so desperately wanted to know. There was a tug, an ache in her chest that indicated her something, something yet to find out. Arlette sat on the bed nearby, where Ember and Cade were quietly sitting. They hadn't spoken a word since all of this chaos started, and Arlette was, somehow, grateful.

"I just want to know what's wrong with me," Arlette confessed, suddenly feeling embarrassed for her outburst earlier. The side effects were definitely starting to wear off.

"I know, dear, though it's...hard, since you're in such a young age."

Arlette was silent, calmly letting her grandmother to continue. Though she had to confess, she was nervous—about what, she didn't know, but she was. Her stomach formed knots and her head pounded, but, surprisingly, Arlette was seemingly calm. Maybe she was used to the feeling, or maybe not. She felt that whatever her grandmother was going to tell her was big...

Arlette could hear her grandma swallow. "Arlette, I don't want you to get upset after I finish,"

"I won't," Arlette promised.

It seemed as if her grandma was finding a way on how to start. Which was something very much rare. She was quiet for a moment before she started.

"We're an...unique family, Arlette," she said carefully. "Our ancestors were different."

Ancestors. Arlette didn't know a single thing about her ancestors. No one had bothered to talk about them all these years. Not even when her family came together to tell great stories of the past. They talked about those amazing, happy, sappy, and wistful legends. Where everything was laughs and rainbows and happily ever afters. Where love was poured out from the heart and happiness was a daily doctrine to the soul. Where the streets weren't infected with corrupted minds and dark souls. Where everything was perfect. But this was reality. And reality was a weight, a reminder, that no life was perfect and that everyone's mind was clouded with fears, sins, and everything else that kept anyone from ever being at peace.

And Arlette felt, and perhaps knew, that her ancestors' story was no happy story. She could be wrong. But then again, her heart was telling her other- wise.

"My grandmother was a witch who married a foreign man of an unkno wn...specie." Her grandmother spoke slowly as her words sank in Arlette's mind. A witch? "He had no identity when it came to where he was origi- nally from. He was not a warlock, a healer, a mind-reader, or of royalty..."

She trailed. "He grew up in a shelter, said someone had left him on the steps there." Arlette didn't know what this had to do with her, but regardless, she listened.

Arlette sensed her mother as she stepped out of the room.

"When he was introduced to the family by my grandmother, Griselda, he wasn't of very much liking to her parents. They said he gave off strange vibes and spirits and assumed he had to be some sort of dark angel or elemental that pulled and toyed with dark forces. But Griselda did not care and nevertheless, married him."

Arlette arched her back, wondering where this was leading.

"Griselda's parents were afraid her children might be carriers of whatever their father was, or worse: become just like their father. But her children were...normal. Just a slight gift for accomplishing magic but not anything out of the usual."

She could feel her grandma hesitate the slightest bit, before continuing.

"Though...her children's children were...wild." she paused. Arlette frowned. Her grandma was now talking about one of her parents. "They had too many unknown abilities at once, and they were immensely noticeable for their bright, fiery eyes and hair. My mother was one of six children," she paused again, taking a deep breath.

Arlette took this opportunity to talk. "What kind of abilities?" she was so painfully curious.

"It differed as each child was born. My mother's brother, Bruce, was able to read minds, control the weather—he also had incredible strength and speed. Her sister, Mirna, was able to control the time; she could go back in the past or in the future, she could also control ice and breathe underwater. My mother could control plants, also make people do whatever she pleased just by speaking...was able to heal others, and she could also control fire. All six of them had different abilities. They had more than that, but they were unknown."

Wow... Arlette tried to speak, but she couldn't. This was just—too much. Regardless, she let every bit of information astonishly crawl in into her mind. Why hadn't they talked about this before?

"And Griselda tried everything, everything for her children to be as normal as everyone else. But they were just so untamable, they held too much things in their hands and they couldn't control it. Her children were soon hidden and taught to control themselves before more people started noticing that there was something not right. Griselda's husband never mentioned knowing anything about why their children were born the were they were, and Griselda never asked for none.

My mother learned to retain herself like all her siblings did. And they lived as normal as a dysfunctional family could after that. When my mother was old enough, she married a guardian. It was meant to pass on to me or your mother. But when it didn't, we feared the worse,"

"It was passed on to me..." Arlette murmured, everything finally seeming to click.

"And your sisters," her grandmother added. "Though Cade has it only by the slightest bit."

Cade groaned when her grandma said the last part, but remained silent.

There was a lot to take in. And Arlette just let her mind wonder, not before her grandmother disturbed her thoughts.

"But it's bad," her grandma said, as if she was frightened. "And we can't risk it."

Something in Arlette fluttered anxiously.

"The forces..." Arlette whispered, remembering when she was healing Aaron, how desperately she pulled forces.

"Yes..." she said sadly, knowing exactly what Arlette was talking about. "There's only a sparse group of the fae here and there that know about...us, and they all believe that such great powers come from evil."

And Arlette once again, let her mind grasp around this information. They didn't think, they believed, which was worse. And evil, no matter the place, person, or circumstances, was meant to be destroyed. Arlette's stomach twisted at the realization of all of this.

All along, all her family had been doing was hide. Hide from who they were—from the judging eyes. "You shouldn't have done that. You don't know what you're provoking against all of us." her mother's voice taunted her with the weight of truth that her words held.

Every warning, precaution, and advice Arlette was given all these years suddenly made sense.

"I can do many things," said Ember casually, as if to lighten up the gloomy mood. Arlette turned to her, curiosity itching in. "Besides manipulating minds, I can also control the earth and make things float."

Arlette was surprised. All these years living together and she didn't know this of Ember. "Really?"

"Yeah, and I can throw things around without even touching them."

Before Arlette could say anything, Cade cut in.

"I can only control plants like grandma's mom." Cade wasn't sad, but she wasn't happy about it either.

"Why didn't anyone tell me about it?" Arlette felt betrayed. Her voice laced with vague pain. And she talked to no one in particular.

"We believe you're the most powerful one, Arlette." Ember replied. "You have this...I don't know...presence that just pours off something." Arlette blinked. "And you are the youngest one in our family. We couldn't expose you to let your powers come up to the surface, when all we're trying to do is stay deep inside sea."

And her family knowing how curious Arlette was, they knew they couldn't trust her with this.

Ember continued, surprising Arlette with her next words. "Haven't you noticed? Well, felt it? When you're going through deep emotions like anger and happiness, your hair looks brighter and more furious." Ember paused. "I've come to think you're able to control fire...or ice."

Arlette was astonished. She'd never come to think of it—sure she felt this prickly, weird sensation when she went through emotions, but she'd always thought it was part of feeling the way she was feeling, not something beyond it all.

Her mind started to bloat with questions. What else was she able she do besides heal? Was there more people like her? Were they all in danger right now?

Arlette remembered the maid talking about her—about her hair... What did she know? Arlette wondered. But most of all, what was he? The strange man her grandma's grandmother married. She felt that was a question that would never be answered.

"Does father know of this?" Arlette didn't know what else to ask.

"Of course," said Ember, and Arlette pursed her lips, wondering what her father thought of this when he discovered what her family was hiding—retraining their powers.

There was still one question that lingered tauntingly in her mind. In fact, there was a lot of questions about this that taunted her mind.

"Why is mom so upset every time I use my, uh...abilities?" The word was still foreign and uncommon in Arlette's lips.

Her grandma scraped the chair closer to Arlette, as if getting closer to her would make it any better. "She herself believes our powers come from evil, and she's just frightened of what people might see and say." Her grandma talked so calmly, serene. As if they were in the gardens, in pure daylight, sipping fancy tea. "Also, if you do it enough times, you won't be able to control your other abilities; you should have around four or five, sometimes more."

Well, that makes sense. Arlette thought, even though her own mother thought her family carried an evil burden with them.

She nodded, understanding, and then Ember said, "I've always wanted to see what you're capable of doing, but of course mom is hysterical about it." Ember was disappointed. "I've learned control mine, even when I use them all."

This was all too new for Arlette. Truth be told, she was blindly stunned. But she also felt utterly betrayed. And the casualty of the way her grandma and Ember talked about it didn't make it any better—they were trying their best to justify the reason why they did not tell Arlette about it. And once again, like always, she was the one untrusted by her family. Arlette couldn't blame them though, she had given them enough reason to.

"I can teach you, if you want." Ember added.

Arlette's ears perked up, despite her thoughts.

---

a/n: This is sort of a filler. OK. Peace. :)

- nessie xoxo

Blind Beauty | 16

D edication goes to SwirlingColours because she became my 600th follower (so long ago ugh)!

MADE SOMETHING--------->

Chapter Dieciseis

"Absolutely not," interrupted her grandma, slight shock lacing through her voice. "There's no way either of you are going to practice your abilities, much less in the palace!" She scoffed. "You got to be out of your mind."

Ember sighed. "But grandma—"

"But grandma nothing, Ember. There are great dangers in this palace. Faes that have preying eyes and big mouths. You know that." Her grandma's voice sounded disappointed, like they both should definitely know better.

Arlette sighed silently. It was true. They couldn't risk themselves like that. No one knew of their abilities. No one should.

But...

Aaron.

He knew what Arlette was capable of doing so far. Yet Arlette was somehow sure that he wouldn't expose her like that. Arlette knew he would do anything but betray her.

"You can't trust anyone. Not even your own shadow," added her grandma.

But Arlette knew she could trust Aaron. There was no question to that.

Under all these thoughts there was but one question that made her skin prickle and her eyes burn. She didn't know if to ask. Maybe she was afraid of asking, or maybe she was afraid of the answer. But it would be stupid to get her hopes up. After so many shattered things, adding something more to the pile was just out the situation. The question had come crashing to her mind like a wild, restless bird. Fast and confused. Afraid of the question and the answer. But she might as well try.

Arlette swallowed. "Am...I able to heal myself?" She faced her grandma. "My...eyes?"

Arlette wished she hadn't asked. The silence that followed her question was heavy and tense. She shouldn't have asked anything. She was getting too far ahead of herself, just as she had thought. It was true, she had these buried abilities and all, but maybe she should have waited longer to ask. Arlette herself knew that, but she couldn't just pass up the wonder that was eating her senses.

"Oh Arlette, there's the catch." Ember said quietly, her voice poignant. "If you are born with a 'flaw' you can't fix it."

Arlette inhaled and nodded understandably. So much for trying. She knew her fate—her destiny was to be the way it had always been and had to be. She couldn't alter it or change it, but live with it and bear it. And it didn't bother her. It didn't bother her that she couldn't heal herself—her eyes. She was just curious like she had always been. Even though her sister's answer triggered and pulled something at her heart, it was okay. Hiding her feelings was better than let them burst out and let them know how she was feeling about this. Plus, she couldn't truly show her emotions. Not anymore. They would stand out on the outside—something Arlette couldn't let happen.

"I'm sorry, Arlette." her grandma whispered.

Arlette smiled. "It's okay, grandma. I was just curious."

Suddenly, after a few seconds of silence, her grandma took both of hands in hers, shocking Arlette with her next question. "Does he hurt you?" Her voice was worried and a little rushed, like she had it at the tip of her tongue but had forgotten to ask it.

Arlette opened her mouth to answer, but she didn't really know what to say. "I..."

Ember cut in, adding, "Arlette, we can hear your screams. They're distant, but persistent." Then asked, just like her grandma. "Does he hurt you?"

She shook her head, saying, "No,"

To be honest, it was quite complicated, because he did hurt her. He weakened her and confused her, but that was because of herself. She fights back, so that causes it. Arlette noticed that he wasn't quite doing it on purpose, it was just the way he was. Such an abstract and complex way, Arlette thought, somehow luring. She had this silent...pull towards him. It was there since the first day she met him. It had only intensified the night of the "choosing".

Arlette had tried to push it it way. Oh, she had tried hard. But she didn't know how to handle this. Whatever she felt was messing up her escaping plans. There just were too many things on the way. Everything was on the way. Besides, if she did escape, where would she go to? All by herself, without food nor water to get by. Arlette shook her head, just another stupid fantasy, she thought.

Her grandma gripped her hands harder. "Arlette, you don't have to lie to us—"

"I'm not, grandma."

"Then, can you explain to me your screams?"

"I was trying to escape. He stopped me. I screamed."

"You were trying to what?!" her grandma let go of her hands. Arlette was glad.

Arlette sighed.

"And where were you going?" Asked her grandma accusingly.

"I don't know, grandma, okay? I just wanted to leave." Arlette was getting tired of her questions.

Now Ember was the one asking questions. "What did I tell you about escaping, Arlette? Are you crazy?"

Arlette got off the bed and started walking towards the door, tired of the pestering and accusing questions. Tired of everything.

"Where do you think you're going, Arlette?"

Arlette stopped, slowly turning around. "I'll come back when you can handle this situation." She said. "See grandma, I'm not five years old anymore, so when you stop overreacting, we can talk about what is happening to me while you enjoy your time here." then she grabbed the door handle and walked out, slamming the door behind her.

She could hear her grandma and Ember call her name, but Arlette ran. She ran frustrated, confused, and angry. They certainly didn't know how she was feeling or going through, and that just tricked with her mind. Weren't they supposed to support her? Wasn't that what family was supposed to do? Arlette didn't know anymore. Everything was falling apart so fast. Tears burned her eyes, but wouldn't let them fall. She couldn't. She had already promised it to herself.

Arlette tripped, not focusing where she was going, but she gritted her teeth and kept going. Where was her father? Arlette needed him so much right now. He was the only one who truly listened to her. But they had lately become quite detached of each other, and that only frightened Arlette. She didn't want to lose the only person that understood her. Oh what she would give right now just to talk to him.

She suddenly bumped hard against someone's back, making her stumble and fall back. The person grunted, while Arlette whimpered silently at the hard thud against her butt.

"Miss?" the voice was surprised and Arlette could be almost sure that it was the guardian that had brought her to her mother. He took her hand in his and pulled her up. "Are you alright?"

Arlette nodded her head quickly. "Yes, I'm fine."

☐   ☐   ☐   ☐   ☐   ☐   ☐

Beast's P.O.V.

"Oh, darlin'." Her face resembled pity as her big eyes grazed over his pumping veins. "Such a shame that you were given more time. You had but mere days! Now this is not going to be as fun." Simone pouted her lips innocently, her hands running over his collarbone down to his torso. "Your veins are darker. You have maybe a couple of weeks left, which is not much may I say..." Simone snapped her eyes toward his. She cocked her head to the side. "Hmm, I wonder why."

He stepped back, away from her touch—away from her. It made him sick.

"Simone..." he said quite threateningly.

"Yes, my darling?"

Anger boiled from his insides. "What are you doing here?" He growled. His voice was thunderous and ominous.

The Prince was tired and angry of her sudden appearances. She herself knew that all he wanted to do was kill her. Every time he saw her, he was but a string away from slamming her against the wall and snap her neck. Besides, he wasn't quite fond of the fact that she had ripped two of his attires into shreds in the past weeks.

"What? Now I can't visit what's left of the one who was once my lover?" But she didn't let him answer. Sighing contemplatingly, she said. "Oh, you remember those wild nights? Hot summer days and foolish stories..." She smiled sickly sweet, the memories taunting him and scratching his mind. "We were so happy, so carefree..." They truly were.

"Simone, not again." he warned. He did remember those nights, and he could say they were the best ones. Beautiful days to remember. But not anymore. They were just an illusion of something that could've once been called love. Plus, it was so long ago that he had forgotten he once was normal at all. Reminding him of them were just like slamming daggers through his heart. Something inside him screeched.

But Simone continued. "How you carried me up the stairs when I was tired. How we used to ride horses till the sun went down." She came closer. "And you gave me everything and anything that I wanted...but then, I made a mistake…and you…you went mad." She looked down, fidgeting with her dress, acting as innocent as a doll.

"I went mad?!" He asked incredulously, rage erupting like a impatient volcano. The trees around them rustled restlessly. The Prince came closer to her as he lowered his voice. She gave several steps back. "Simone, look at me. Just look at me." he demanded. "You are the one who went mad. You are the one who did this to me." Simone was toying with his emotions and he knew that. They both did, and Simone was enjoying this like she always did.

Simone looked at him with a flat look upon her face. "You deserved it—"

The Prince slammed her against a tree, his big hand around her pale neck. The words hurt him more than he'd expected.

Simone let out a cry that resonated through the whole forest. She closed her eyes, then opened them again, inhaling sharply, and almost instantly, she was just staring at him with serene, calm, ode eyes. "Don't you remember, my love? If I die, you die." she smiled at him, her lips crimson red and pearly white teeth shining under the moonlight.

He remembered.

The Prince let go of her slowly, stepping away from her. Simone ran both of her hands down her dress, dusting it off, then she looked at him, and that might just had been the first time in a century that she had a sincere look upon her face.

"I loved you, Vince. I truly did. The situation just got out of hand. But if I could go back, I would do it again. I would throw the curse at you. A thousand times over." And then, as graceful as a butterfly, she disappeared through the trees.

a/n: Hello guys. Before you kill me for the short chapter, I want to apologize for not updating in OVER A MONTH. Believe me, I could hear your cry. But I was just so, so, so, so choked up with school you don't even know. I guess the chapter is short because I'm in the point where I'm figuring out some things in the story. (meaning we're getting closer to the end *CRIES*)

On another hand, lately, I've seen some comments here and there that it's like hearing nails dig and crawl on chalkboard. Believe me guys, I'm doing this right now because i don't want several bad comments to turn into a ton.

I love you all but some things just have to be pointed out.

That being said, I will not, I repeat, will not tolerate any degrading comments or opinions. Don't tell me how to write my story. Remember that there's a thin line between critiquing someone's story and degrading it. I know what's happening in the story, I know why things happen. I'm the author. I'm the one taking time out of my day to write. I don't get paid for this—not saying that I need to be, but I'm just saying. Dumb comments make me wanna slam my head against my keyboard. And I hate to point out this, because I sound like a whiny little girl, but my patience is one that runs thinner than a string. And um yeah. Please don't test it. I consider myself a nice person (lol) so please just don't.

Here are some questions that people have been having lately (since the beginning maybe) about the story. (You do not have to read this if you don't have any confusions):

How old is Arlette?

18.

Does Aaron know Arlette is blind?

He does. But it is not revealed in the story. Don't ask why.

Why is Arlette able to control her abilities at a young age, but her ancestors couldn't?

I think it's self explanatory. Arlette didn't know about her abilities in the first place and her family always told her to not do anything reckless since a young age. And every time she did, she was being warned for it. Plus, she thought her family was as normal as a family in the Fae Lands could get.

Are her abilities going to be a big part of the story?

Not necessarily. But they will come up from time to time when necessary.

Why the plot twist?

I felt like it. Even though it's not really a "plot twist".

Also, please don't let any of this hold you from commenting. Comment all you want, just don't degrade me or my story. Thank you for understanding.

- nessie xoxo

p.s sorry for any mistakes. This is not edited.

p.s.s If you have any more questions, just ask!

Dedicated to AlleyMcAllister for the gorgeous banner on the side!

Chapter Diecisiete

Arlette was getting tired of her constant fallings in the halls. She could almost laugh at the many times she'd fallen. Though really not understanding how anyone could fall so many times.

"Where were you heading, my lady?" the guardian asked expectantly.

Arlette was blank. Where was she heading? She didn't even know. "Uh..."

"You're not supposed to run the halls—"

"No, I know. I just needed some fresh air," she said quickly, smiling to reassure him. She did need fresh air, she needed to get away from her grandma, from her mom, from everybody. Arlette felt suffocated, like things were piling up inside of her. She wanted things to go smoother than this. Way smoother now that she thought of it. None of this was supposed to happen. Arlette wasn't supposed to come to this place and be locked up for weeks. She wasn't supposed to meet the Prince. She wasn't supposed to have dreams about this morbid woman, or be chosen by Fate. Arlette wasn't supposed to have abilities or be anything out of the ordinary.

Arlette wasn't supposed to feel anything for the Beast. But there was something. A sting, a prickle tugging against her very soul. It was scary, yet fascinating. Despite her being beyond terrified of him, somehow, he was always in her thoughts, like a wolf lurking in the shadows, waiting, waiting, waiting.

Arlette felt like she could have a mental breakdown.

"Miss?" Arlette jumped a little at the sudden disturbance of her thoughts. "Are you hearing anything of what I'm saying?"

Arlette felt guilty for that. "No. Please forgive me. I..."

"Miss, don't apologize. It's alright," he said sincerely. "I was but informing you that the Prince wants to see you at his study."

Can her day just get anymore interesting?

Something in her stomach thrashed.

Arlette was trying to keep it together. "Oh yes, of course."

"Very well then," the guardian said. Arlette made a move to go, but the guardian then said, "Come, miss, allow me to escort you there."

He stood next to her, and Arlette slid her hand through the gap between his elbow and rib cage, and rested it on his forearm, allowing him to guide her.

The walk was silent. But Arlette didn't want silence.

"What's your name?" she asked casually. Arlette liked knowing people's names even though she considered it a small bad habit of hers.

But the guardian didn't seem bothered by her question. "Why, my name is Alfonso, miss."

Arlette nodded. "Alfonso... Very unique," she said truthfully.

"Thank you, my lady."

"Arlette. You can call me Arlette,"

"Oh, miss, I don't think the Prince or the King would like that. There are very, very strict rules here, specifically about that."

Arlette didn't know that. "There are?"

"I'm afraid so,"

They stayed silent after that. The silence engulfing them both. It wasn't uncomfortable or overwhelming, but nice and peaceful. Arlette understood that the guardians had limits, and she couldn't make him cross them.

□

Arlette felt that they got there way too fast. It was strange that knots were forming in her stomach at the thought that she'd be meeting him once again. But Arlette wasn't really in her best state. All the things that happened today had her feeling a little unwell.

Very unwell.

And not too soon, the guardian was knocking very gently on the door, indicating that they were certainly here.

"Come in," said the voice on the other side. That voice that made the hairs on Arlette's arms and neck rise up. That voice that echoed in the pits of her mind. That voice that horrified her and blew her senses away. His voice.

The guardian slowly dropped his arm, opening the door for Arlette.

She turned to him before stepping in. "Thank you,"

"My pleasure," he bowed his head—Arlette could feel it—then closed the door behind her once she was inside.

As always, his presence screeched of power and authority and darkness and everything he was every time she was near him. The feeling had become all too familiar to Arlette. She didn't know if to be glad or frightened. But then again, there was always something more to it. Like a gentle pull. She just couldn't figure it out.

Arlette walked several steps forward before stopping.

She didn't know where in the study he was. The room was well filled with his scent. It felt like he spent most of his time here. It was ample too, and warm. She could hear the persistent but distant crackling of the wood in fire nearby. Arlette liked the sound. It soothed her explosive senses.

Why would he want her here for?

Arlette hugged herself, despite the warmness of the room, as long seconds ticked by.

"Are you alright?" His voice was surprisingly calm and that somehow shocked and angered Arlette.

"Why wouldn't I be?" she dropped her arms to the side, clenching her fists. She didn't know why that question infuriated her so much.

There was silence for a moment.

Then he said, "You're not, I can feel it."

Arlette froze, but stayed quiet. She didn't know what to say. She didn't know if what he was saying was true. But it was true. Arlette was not okay. There was too much going on. She didn't know what to think, what to be believe in, what to do anymore. Arlette was lost. Completely and utterly lost. She'd said she'd made up her mind. But she hadn't. Arlette needed someone. She needed her dad.

The Prince wasn't near her or too far off either. But she could feel his piercing eyes breaking through her soul.

"I'm fine." was all she said, not having any strength to argue.

He walked towards her and out of instinct, Arlette backed away.

But there was something inside of her that regretted it.

"Your father..." The Prince started saying. He was careful using his words.

That got her attention, if it wasn't already all on him.

"What about my father?" Arlette interrupted quickly, walking back towards him. Did something happen to him? Arlette's eyes stung with tears at the thought, but she pushed them away harshly, trying not to get ahead of herself.

Now they were close. Close enough.

"He's very ill,"

Ill?

"My guardians found him in the Dark Forest this morning. It seems that he was bitten by something there."

No.

He couldn't be serious.

Arlette could feel her heart tear into shreds as shock and realization dawned in. "Bitten? He was bitten?" Arlette couldn't believe it. "But my father knows how dangerous the Dark Forest is. Why would he be there?" She asked herself, walking backwards until her back hit the wall.

The Prince was silent.

Silence sank in.

Arlette's head snapped up, her voice quieter and almost cracking. "Why would you tell me this? Does my mother know?"

"No one knows. The first thing Eric said when he woke up was to not tell anyone." He walked towards her once again. His presence very strong, but Arlette didn't care. That was the last thing that bothered her right now.

"But you."

The Prince was dangerously close now as Arlette rested her head on the wall. But she didn't have the strength to move away. Where would she move to anyway? She was trapped. And as seconds ticked by, she could feel the heat radiating off of him, and his breathing delicately fanning her face. Arlette liked the feeling, but his closeness was getting to her. She felt a good stingy sensation all over. It wrapped all around her like a snake, overwhelming her. Her hands prickled, compelled with the craving to touch the art that was carved on him. The gentle pull she'd been feeling suddenly became stronger, more powerful and unbearable, it ripped through her mind and senses, luring her body in. Arlette's mind screamed a word that was too embarrassing for her to even think. Her breath quickened, suddenly experiencing a destructive feeling of deja vu.

She placed her hand on his chest, very slowly and carefully. The small action making her body feel like it was bursting into flames. "Please," she whispered, almost speechless by the overwhelming feeling he gave her. "Let me see him,"

□   □   □   □   □   □   □

Beast's P.O.V.

If only she knew how much he wanted to touch her. She was so innocent and pure, he'd been careful to even look at her the wrong way. He was a poisonous and deadly ink, she was beautiful and pure, like freshly fallen snow. He didn't want to taint her with his scarred hands or thoughts.

Seeing her so broken made his hollow heart flinch. But it was harder for him to tell her. To see how her brilliant, blinding light dimmed ominously. To see how hard those news hit her. It was like someone had ripped out her very soul. She turned pale and weak, like she herself was bitten. He knew how she was feeling. The bond was being tied into knots—was getting stronger, bigger. They both could feel it.

He had gotten near her, because he wanted to comfort her. Because that was what she needed. He'd thought of caressing her flushed cheeks and devouring her. But he was a monster. A monster with a past. Yet the ardent tension between them was telling otherwise. Her vibrant orbs glowed as she took quick breaths and closed her eyes briefly, trying to fight off the feeling. That just made something inside him twist with devastating want and need.

And then she placed her hand on his chest, keeping him but a string away from taking her right then and there.

"Please," she had whispered. He liked how she talked—only for him to hear. Her voice was soft like silk, yet at the same time rich and filled with every emotion possible. "Let me see him."

And she did.

❑   ❑   ❑   ❑   ❑   ❑   ❑

Arlette's P.O.V.

They had gone to another room, on another side of the palace. Arlette didn't know if it was only her but it smelled heavily of herbs and sickness .Were she heard innocent whispers and the word death hung in the ceiling like squeaky light bulbs. Were cold, rough chills racked down Arlette's spine and made her really think about her father's condition.

The Prince hadn't said anything about his condition, but Arlette already had an idea just of how carefully and precisely he told her. But also, not only that, she could feel it. Arlette could feel how death had its arms open, waiting to embrace her father. Arlette felt nauseous at the thought, tears at the verge of falling, mentally praying for him.

Her father was a strong and brave man. He'd done any and every job just so that his family won't miss a meal. He was the only person that saw the good side to everything. That did not overreact or turned things down like her mother or grandmother. He believed everything was possible as long as he believed in it. Arlette was ignorant. She had been ignorant. She got so caught up in her own things, she wasn't realizing that she slowly was growing apart from her father, only now when he was in such a horrible state... Her chest tightened, guilt sinking in like a heavy rock.

A door opened and Arlette could smell her dad's familiar scent, reminding her of her home in the village. The village that was burned down by Lord knows what.

Arlette couldn't help it, a sob escaped from her lips as she stepped inside.

Nobody needed to guide her, she knew exactly where her father was.

Arlette sensed as the Prince stayed behind, perhaps giving her space.

"Oh, father..." she whispered as she neared the bed, quickly grabbing his hand in hers.

His hand was freezing.

She squeezed it gently and could feel as her father took a deep breath. "Arlette, my dear, you came," his voice was croaky and drained as if he was unbearably tired, but Arlette could feel the relief he felt.

"How could I not…" she said quietly as tears ran down her face mercilessly. "What happened? How did this happen?"

Her father, Eric, coughed. He coughed madly and horribly. Arlette turned her face away, waiting patiently for him to talk, feeling a crush in her stomach.

"I…" he started, his breathing uneven, "I was on my way to the palace…" he was panting and Arlette could feel his hand starting to sweat. "And…som eone—something dragged me from the path…and into the Dark Forest," he said tiredly. "I tried to run away…but…it bit me hard," then he added after a couple of moments, "it was powerful and strong."

Arlette frowned through the tears. "Father, you said someone dragged you in?" That was strange. Why would anyone want to go inside the Dark Forest, and much less put their lives at risk dragging her father in? And it couldn't have been the forest itself because the forest doesn't drag people in. It leads people in.

"It was something or someone…I don't remember. They were speaking in a strange language. I don't know what they were saying but the thing sounded angry."

What could it had been?

Arlette had no idea.

"We found him at the edge of the Dark Forest—we believe he tried to drag himself out," someone said. Another guardian probably.

Arlette didn't even notice there was someone else with them.

"But why into the Dark Forest?" Arlette asked herself quietly.

The Dark Forest was disturbing and blood-curdling. It fed off anyone's fear, like a nightmare. It was like an illusion, but horribly real. Arlette had heard stories from the Dark Forest. Horrible stories before the Fae began to know how deadly it was. Like the one where a little boy on his way from his friend's cottage had gotten lost. It'd been rumored that he saw a path through the Dark Forest and he'd figured it was his way home.

Tragically wrong.

The little boy had this odd fear toward frogs. He'd entered the forest and nothing happened, other than how distracting it looked. Everything was black. The trees, the branches, the leaves, the ground, everything...but when he was nearing the clearing where everything was clear and green and sunny, the dark, thick branches of the trees started to snake together, covering the exit. The little boy panicked. He looked back, thinking about going back to his friend's cottage and staying there until his mother started looking for him, but there was no going back. The path that had led him in was banished, and all he could see was black. The little boy started getting scared. Adding to his torture, he started hearing noises. Familiar, frightening noises. Frog noises.

The little boy started breathing hard as devastating fear started creeping in. He called for help, but his small voice became restricted. The noises got near and the ground started to shake with hard thumps. The little boy started to run as fast he could. He ran and ran, and a sticky gooey thing started leaking from the trees, dripping to his head, down his body. He was soaking wet of it. He sobbed horribly, knowing what it was. He tripped every time the ground shook, making him fall hard on the floor. The frog shrieked. The little boy looked back, seeing the abominable, humongous thing right behind him, lashing its long tongue out.

Fear was winning. He became tired. Fear was sucking, draining, his fragile soul. After all, that was what it did every time it won. It mercilessly slurped the life out of people.

The little boy fell. But he stayed on the ground, sweaty with tears in his eyes, too tired to get up.

He mumbled the same sweet nothings his mother used to whisper to him as his flushed face became pale and his eyes dead.

The first time Arlette heard this story, it hit her hard. And it still did. It was tragic and horrific.

"We have to tell grandma," Arlette said as realization dawned in.

Eric became alarmed. "No! Don't tell anything to your grandmother or Lena,"

Arlette frowned, "Why? They must be really worried," Arlette couldn't understand what was wrong with her father.

"No…" he let out an exhausted breath, "far from it."

---

a/n: Okay so I kind of don't like this chapter. Eh, it was okay. But I apologize for the long wait! I'm not even going to promise you that I'll update sooner, because I don't even know if I will. I'm just really thankful that you guys have stuck by despite my broken promises.

Anyways, this is not edited.

- nessie xoxo

Blind Beauty | 18

Chapter Dieciocho

Arlette was beyond shocked.

Far from it?

She was lost of words, "What..."

"Arlette, my dear, your mother is...vicious," he whispered the last word, as if afraid someone might hear him. "She demands the power that I do not have," he said softly.

"Father, what are you talking about? What are you saying?"

Arlette felt as he became alarmed once again, as if he'd just realized something.

The Prince was here.

He coughed, then he said, barely loud enough for the Prince to hear, "Your Highness, if it is not much to ask, I wish to speak with my daughter alone," her father said the words with all due and honorable respect, it really showed how much he valued the Prince, but Arlette felt she couldn't turn back and face the Prince. She just couldn't even if she should have.

The Prince said nothing, but Arlette heard the door creak open and then seconds later, close.

Her father released a relieved breath.

She still couldn't understand. "What is it, father?"

Arlette could hear as her father began to have a hard time breathing. "Arlette, there are some things you should know," he explained quietly. Then he said, "Your mother and I are no longer together,"

Arlette's eyes widened and her body became stiff at the sudden news. Regardless, her father continued to talk forcibly, "Since we got here,"

"But why?" was all she could ask.

He sighed shallowly. "It just wasn't...working out, my dear." He drew a long breath. "After we came to the palace, she was so...infatuated with finding out who you really were—finding out who was the man your grandma's grandma married...And to find out she had to negotiate and do reckless things and decisions. I didn't want to have any part in it. All of our arguments and disputes always came down to that one man," He coughed uncontrollably, groaning painfully, but regardless, continued, adding, "she has just lost all affection towards me,"

Arlette couldn't believe it. Her mother had never showed any signs of such obsession. She was always just very cautious about Arlette and her sisters but nothing as far as negotiations and other things.

Her father released a raw whimper, shifting his weight roughly.

Arlette knew this was not normal. She became alarmed. "What's wrong?"

"It's just pain, my dear, that's all," he croaked. "Can you pass me the bowl on the table behind you, to your left?" Arlette nodded quickly, letting go of her father and turning around, grabbing the bowl from the table. He coughed harder that time, driving Arlette to the verge of breaking down. She didn't though, and instead quickly passed him the bowl.

He spat roughly in it, followed by around of dry, painful coughs.

Arlette's hands trembled. She could recognize that smell anywhere. "Fat her...you're coughing up blood." She said softly, quietly.

"I know," he said, as if accepting his destiny. His voice wasn't happy, or sad, or disappointed, just...accepting.

Arlette's eyes filled with tears. How could her father just accept this? This was no honorable way for this to come to an end. As her mind was quickly scrambled with thoughts, she could also feel as blood oozed out of him from somewhere—she didn't know, it was too overwhelming; blood always was.

"Father..." Arlette whispered, her face covered in tears. This broke her heart more than anything else. "You're bleeding."

"My right shoulder," was all he said.

She nodded, running her hand slowly from his stomach, up to his collarbone, and the then carefully to his shoulder. She rubbed softly. Her father grunted. The wound had a thick, rugged bandage protecting it, but it didn't stop the flowing blood from coming out in great, terrifying portions.

When Arlette removed her hand, it was soaking wet.

She stepped back as the blood slid up her fingertips and to the floor in thick, red droplets. The smell was now suffocating, engulfting.

"I-I need to call s-someone..." she stammered in tears, horrified. Her body trembled as cold waves of fear crashed down her spine and into her bones. Just when she was about to run to the door, her father grabbed her hand. He didn't say anything—maybe he couldn't—he just gripped on Arlette's hand like his life depended on it.

Arlette gripped his hand too, but she knew if she stayed long her father wouldn't probably make it. She felt a pang in her heart.

"I haven't finished telling you," her father croaked.

What?

Through her unbelievable shock and fear, Arlette tried to reassure her father, "You can always tell me later—"

"No," he coughed. "It would be too late."

Arlette shook her head as she restrained sobs from escaping her lips. But as if it was Fate herself, a thought quickly crashed Arlette's mind, and she saw hope again.

"F-father...I can fix you..." she smiled through the tears. How could she not have thought of it earlier? She had her abilities now; she was no ordinary Fae. That realization lifted her heart. "I just need to—"

"No! You will do no such thing," he gasped.

And everything just crashed down again. "But father—"

"No, my dear, I don't want you to. My fate shall be what it is—you shouldn't change it."

"But it's not to die!" she said desperately, tears running down her face mercilessly. Her father didn't deserve to die this way. It was just unbearable, surreal.

"Just...let me finish, my dear." he said breathlessly, and Arlette nodded, granting her father his wish. "Do not trust anyone. Ever."

"I won't," she reassured him quickly, taking both of his hands in hers.

"Don't let them wash your head with the idea that you are evil…you are not, my dear. You are light. You are brighter than the sun. You are grace and beauty and goodness."

His words ripped through Arlette's soul, tearing her apart. He was saying goodbye.

Just when Arlette was about to say something, the door was slammed open.

Everything happened so fast.

A man began shouting, "The healer! Bring me the healer!"

She could hear as men and women hurried about in the room, all surrounding her father. But she just stood there, gripping his father's hands, not believing what was really happening.

Someone grabbed her, "My lady, you can't be here,"

But Arlette didn't react, she didn't move, didn't blink, didn't do a thing. She just stood there as the world spun around her. The person said something else, but all the commotion became muffled and distant as understanding dawned in.

She could've fixed her father.

He would've been fine.

They would've been happy.

But Arlette didn't, all because he didn't want her to.

Funny how the opportunity of her father being healed was so close, that he could've almost reach into and touch it, but his acceptance was closer. If that made any sense.

After that, Arlette didn't know if she fainted, or was asleep, or even dead. She just felt herself gone. Her strength had worn out—she couldn't do it anymore.

□

Arlette wasn't quite sure where she was. Well, she did know where she was, it was just strange how it felt to be here. She was back in her village, in her meadow. Her favorite meadow. Though it felt as if someone had just made a copy of the original one. The place felt unreal, like she was just trying so hard to remember it, it became some sort of illusion.

She was sitting under the huge oak tree. The wind made the leaves rustle and her hair flow. Everything was so peaceful. Like it had always been. She heard the daisies and birds chirp harmoniously, reminding her of home. Arlette could also hear the small children laughing in the distance.

But she felt something off. Utterly off.

Following her instincts, Arlette got on her feet, the feeling of the soft grass beneath her feet indicating that she was barefoot, and started walking.

As she walked towards her cottage, she began to smell smoke coming from there. Her heart began to beat erratically. And then she heard the screams. The agonizing and long screams. Screams from her mother, from her sisters, from her grandmother, from her father...

Desperation took over, and her breath quickened, which caused her to run as fast as she could towards the front door. The screams got louder and the smell became stronger. Accompanied with the gory, rotten, and powerful smell of frying flesh.

She slammed the door open and everything went silent.

There was no fire, no smell of burnt flesh, or sickening screams. Everything was just as peaceful as it was outside in the meadow.

Arlette stepped inside, but she couldn't hear anyone. The house was empty.

Her heart sank.

"Did you miss me?" Arlette jumped at the grisly, familiar voice. She could feel as knots formed in her stomach.

Not again...

"What are you doing here?" Arlette asked, outraged. This strange woman was getting on her nerves. Arlette knew that all she screamed was danger. Danger was the last thing Arlette wanted to be in.

"I just felt like visiting you, dear." she said in a sickly sweet voice. Then she added absentmindedly, "You should listen to your father. Trusting is for the weak."

Arlette gasped, "How did you—"

"I know everything, darlin'." She chuckled maliciously. "I know and I see everything,"

Arlette opened her mouth to talk, but the woman beat her, "Though I don't agree with him on the other part," she said, clarifying, "that you're not evil, that is. Because you are."

Her words sank in deep and hurt Arlette more than she had expected. Fury boiled inside of her. "I'm not evil!" A strong wind picked up as she said those words, and Arlette could feel as something powerful engulfed her.

It frightened her.

The woman laughed. "Oh, Arlette, my dear, that was perfect. Even though this is just a dream, that small action was marvelous."

"I'm not evil..." Arlette kept whispering again and again.

"Anyone with the kinds of abilities that you have is evil, you do not make the exception, my dear."

"I'm not evil, I'm not evil..." Arlette kept whispering. "I'm light, not darkness."

The woman ignored her. "You should wake up. You have been sleeping all evening and night. The sun is about to rise, and the ball is tonight," she said, seemingly excited.

Arlette's head snapped toward the woman's silky voice. "The ball?" Arlette had forgotten about it.

"Yes." Arlette could sense the woman's smile. "The ball is tonight. And prepare yourself, darlin', because I have a gift for you. You will have it by tomorrow,"

"What gift?"

"Ah," she laughed. "It's a surprise."

Blind Beauty | 19

Credits to contorted for the gorgeous banner on the side!

Chapter Diecinueve

Arlette woke up startled, with fast breaths and sweaty palms.

And hot tears.

Fear crashed at her spine like merciless rocks.

There's no way that woman could give her a gift, right? She was only a dream. Dreams weren't reality.

But then again, she'd say she was once the Prince's lover, which terrified Arlette even more than she had expected.

And suddenly something clicked, and questions started to rattle in.

Was she the same woman who threw the curse at the Prince? Arlette remembered her mother telling her about an horrible witch throwing a strong curse at him. She itched with curiosity. Who knew. Maybe she was, which put Arlette in great danger and made fear hit her like waves, or maybe not, and she was just one of the women he'd probably encounter. Either of the two, that woman seemed dangerous enough and just the thought of her being a witch petrified Arlette to the point of madness.

But then again, the gift she said she was going to give Arlette didn't seem to have the best of intentions.

In her understanding, gifts were good things. They were items or objects or anything else of value that was meant for good. Why would that woman want to give her a gift after the torture she'd put Arlette in? There has got to be something behind it, Arlette concluded as hysteria made its way slowly to her body, something not right. She was more than just a woman in a dream, she was something else, something evil.

Arlette, without noticing, was sitting at the edge of the bed, letting her hands wander on the familiar bed and letting her thoughts lurk in.

But as thoughts twirled and thrashed themselves against Arlette's mind, something, something more important and stronger and intense wrecked her whole being, making her choke on her own breath.

Her father.

That hideous silence strained in, and the only thing she could hear was how hard her heart started beating in her chest, how she felt all her bones shatter into a million pieces, how her breath got faster, like she was trapped and there was no escape, how a hollowness crowded her heart and smashed it.

Without thinking, she got off the bed, the cold marble floor making the hairs on her arms stand, and practically ran to the door, the emptiness hugging her as tears threatened to fall.

She yanked the door open, and ran outside, only to crash into someone.

"My lady?"

Arlette recognized that voice.

"Elsa…" she sighed, suddenly glad.

Elsa hugged her, and Arlette hugged her back. Intensely, fiercely, like she needed to hang on to something so she wouldn't break into a million pieces on the floor.

They stayed like that for a moment before Arlette found her voice, merely a whisper, "How...is he?"

Elsa didn't respond, she just hugged Arlette tighter, stroking her long hair. Perhaps she didn't hear her.

Arlette opened her mouth to speak again, not before Elsa started talking, "He's...um—" She swallowed, breathing deep. She was having a hard time. "Oh Arlette..." her voice cracked, and she breathed in. "He... didn't make it, dear, he lost too much blood."

Arlette felt everything around her fall to pieces, even herself. She felt like her heart was being mercilessly stabbed, like her soul was abruptly torn apart from her. A heavy, dreadful weight sat on her shoulders, making her legs go weak and her eyes watery with a weird taste in her tongue. And screams, screams, screams everywhere in her mind and a bitterness in the atmosphere. For Arlette, this was one of those times where things felt unreal. Like she was in a dream, but not really. Like these were fantasies and illusions and things you didn't encounter right away. Anomalies in which you only saw and felt in your most deepest and dauntless dreams for them to happen to you. Things that you know cannot happen to you, but by Fate, or curses, they somehow do.

The news hit her hard. Harder than she'd expected.

How could it not? He was her father after all.

Arlette broke down in Elsa's arms. Her sobs and screams of frustration and agony and anger and sorrow echoing in every hallway of the palace. Unforgiving tears wrecked down her face, making her whole body tremble. She screamed again, as if wanting Fate herself to hear her, and she did want Fate to hear her. She wanted Fate to hear her and see how she had hurt her. How unfair and horrible this was, how extremely wrong this was, how terribly and awfully this pained Arlette.

Her miserable sobs never stopped and Elsa just stroked her hair softly, whispering sweet nothings. Arlette's legs were weak, and her only support was Elsa. She was glad Elsa was here.

"The King is willing to postpone the Grand Ball, if that's what you wish," said Elsa softly.

Arlette shook her head softly, picking her up from Elsa's shoulders, but never pulling away. "It's okay." For a split second, Arlette thought about the King, wondering how he had taken these news. He and her father were effectively close and Arlette wondered how he was feeling.

"Are you sure? He can just inform everyone—"

Arlette shook her head once again, finding a mild strength. "No, it's okay, really." she said quietly, adding, "He has been preparing for this day for a long time. I will be fine, I promise."

"As you wish, my dear," Elsa said.

Arlette's sobs were calmed by now, there was only tears streaming down involuntarily and she wished she could go back and talk to her father one more time.

"Does my mother know?" Arlette suddenly asked, merely a broken whisper.

"She does, and so do your sisters and your grandmother."

"Where are they?"

"Downstairs, preparing to eat breakfast."

"Can I go?"

"Of course," Elsa said, "but first, you have to bathe and get ready,"

Arlette and Elsa went back to the room—the Prince's room.

Arlette hadn't noticed until now that it was his all this time. The special softness of the pillows and covers, the overwhelming, familiar and elusive scent of them and the spacious room...nothing, only the familiarity of the bed.

She wondered where the Prince was. Always wondered about him. The thought of him always made her feel strange inside. There was always something so utterly intriguing about the way Arlette thought of him, like there was this longing in her heart that she couldn't quite put her finger on.

Elsa helped Arlette undress and get in the tub, leaving the bathroom only to find her some clothes.

Arlette shifted softly under the warm water. Elsa had scattered petals of roses in the tub, their scent now filing Arlette's nose with comfort. She closed her eyes, breathing deep, pushing the present tears away. She couldn't believe her father was...dead. It was so difficult for her mind to wrap around it, she was still questioning if it was true. But she knew it was. Last time she saw him he was losing blood faster than how rain would fall. Death could be sensed that day, lurking, waiting and waiting and waiting. Arlette sighed with a sadness she couldn't describe.

Not wanting more thoughts to weaken her, she stood up on the tub, then slowly stepped out, the water from her naked and wet body sliding down the floor. Right at that moment, the door opened and Arlette gasped.

"It's just me," Elsa reassured, closing the door behind her and walking towards Arlette, wrapping a towel around her.

"Thank you,"

They stepped out of the bathroom and Arlette began to dress.

Elsa was somewhere in the room. "The maids are busy with the decorations and the dresses and everything for tonight," she said it casually as to start a conversation. And Arlette remembered how one of the maids, Daisy, had excitedly talked about their role in that part.

"It seems they take great honor in doing those things," Arlette said quietly as she smoothed out her simple dress.

"They do. It's a privilege here in the Fae Lands to be able to do that."

Arlette finished brushing her hair and they stepped out of the room, not before Elsa handed her her cane, and went downstairs to the dining room, or one of the dining rooms, who knew?

Arlette could hear her family chatter quietly as if they were afraid someone might be near and hear them.

She felt numb, only wondering if her father's death had affected them as horribly as it had to her. Probably not.

Arlette stepped in and suddenly, everyone went into a dead silence.

"Good morning, dear." her grandmother greeted softly.

"Good morning." Arlette responded solemnly, taking a chair and sitting down.

Her mom suddenly grabbed her hand, sniffling, "Oh Arlette—"

Arlette yanked her hand away from her mother's grip, saying, "Do not touch me," with gritted teeth. She hadn't noticed she'd sat down next to her mother, perhaps her senses were weak and worn out, but if she had, she wouldn't had.

"This has all impact us very hard so we must remain calm," her grandma advised after a moment of silence.

"I am calm." Arlette said, collected, and began to eat.

Ember and Cade were quiet the whole time, just sighing. Arlette wondered what they were thinking.

Moments later, the talking started again, and it was from her mother. Babbling about her father and his death. Every word she said about her father made anger and agony bloom in Arlette's entire being. "I don't understand...how could that happen to him—it just makes no sense...he was coming from his work and then a path—and the Dark Forest...a bite ...blood and blood and blood everywhere—"

"Mom!" Arlette screamed, and the ground trembled beneath them with a force Arlette couldn't describe and suddenly, she was feeling her strength coming back. Her hands and the tip of her fingers prickled with a feeling of electricity and power, they crawled up her arm and her whole body, making her feel vivid and pure and alive. And all this happened in a matter of milliseconds.

Her mother had gasped in pure horror.

"Thank the Lords there are no guardians here," Ember whispered to herself, but Arlette heard her.

"I told you mother, whatever she is can't possibly be good, just look at her hair—"

"And what if I'm not good?" She challenged. "Would you still consider me as your daughter?"

Only two surprised words escapedher lips, "What—Arlette..." But she didn't answer.

Arlette laughed through the sadness she felt. "I know you didn't love father..." she said quietly.

There was a silence.

"I did." Was all she said, and Arlette shook her head. Arlette didn't tell her what her father did though. She didn't want things to get worse. She only told her that she'd known all along that they weren't together, but her mother's only response was silence.

"You're all acting as if this shouldn't hurt us. Like we're made of stones," Arlette whispered, disappointed. She knew how much her family hated to show pain and weakness. It'd been the first time Arlette encounter her mother in such weak state, but she quickly collected herself after Arlette's burst. It seemed that the only who had strong emotions was Arlette, and she was fine with it.

After Arlette was finished, she called for a guardian to guide her to the gardens.

Nobody protested.

---

a/n: And at last, I've updated. Yes, this was difficult to write, and yes I know it's not as exciting but I want to add the best part for last, you know, which will be in the next chapter. *wiggles eyebrows*

I've got to admit guys, my writing became sort of rusty over the two months I wasn't able to write/update. LOL. But it's whatever. I'm back at it now. Sort of. Comment and vote and tell me how much you missed the story/characters!

Much love,

- nessie xoxo

Chapter Veinte

Arlette spent most of the afternoon in the gardens, walking, crying, laughing, singing, thinking...

She needed the time alone. Feeling pressured all the time was pushing her to the edge of insanity. She had missed the feeling of being able to be alone and at peace. Now she could breathe and be herself.

Her fingertips had touched every flower and every plant and tree and every bird in the garden, all of them chirped and hummed, welcoming her. She smiled humming with them. The day was lovely, she could feel it and the birds let her know.

Arlette even met with Phoenix again, the Prince's monstrous wolf. For a moment she thought the wolf was with him. But the wolf was completely alone. Making Arlette's heart throb for some reason. Yet when Phoenix first saw her, he ran to her, making her fall back on the grass, laughing. He licked her face and nudged her, making soft growling noises. She caressed his amazing fur, smiling. She hadn't smiled in what felt like forever, let alone laugh.

After what seemed like hours, Phoenix left without warning. It was like he was suddenly being called, but Arlette didn't hear any voices or noises at all—everything was just as peaceful. That alarmed Arlette a little, but she didn't mind much. Yet, minutes after Phoenix left, Arlette could hear steps approach her. She stood frozen in place.

"Arlette...?"

She found her breath.

"Daisy..." Arlette exhaled.

"Do you know how late you are?" Daisy sounded worried.

Arlette had forgotten the Grand Ball was today. "Uh..."

Daisy sighed. "It's okay, but we must go. You still have to get ready." Then Daisy made strange noise. "But first a bath."

Arlette's lips quirked up slightly, remembering Phoenix, and nodded, following Daisy back inside.

□

When Arlette went back to the room, there were surprisingly a lot of maids. Before she could ask, Daisy explained that all of them will help her get ready. Still, Arlette didn't understand the need for a dozen maids. They all paced around quietly but she could still hear their constant voices. Arlette felt somewhat uncomfortable taking her dress off in front of all of them, so she went to the bathroom instead.

No one seemed to notice, or maybe they didn't want to disturb her, but Arlette didn't mind and quickly got in the tub for the second time today.

The water was very warm and calming. As soon as her body was engulfed in water, she could feel the tension of her body ooze out. A sigh escaped her lips, and she enjoyed how it felt to be this relaxed.

After a good amount of time in the tub, Arlette decided to get out. She stood up, grabbing the towel near her and wrapping it around her body. Stepping out of the tub and walking back into the room, she could hear the intense conversation two maids were having in the corner of the room. For some reason, it annoyed her that they were talking very quietly about her, but Arlette still managed to hear them clearly.

Daisy was by her side in an instant, helping her dry up and get dressed.

Arlette managed to keep up with them, but the maids were effortlessly and smoothly fast, basically dressing her themselves. They complimented the dress, saying it was the most precious and divine dress they'd ever made in a long time. It fitted Arlette perfectly. She ran her hands over it, feeling the soft material carved with symmetrical, delicate designs. It felt beautiful. Arlette liked it. The maids worked with her face then her hair. Instead of putting her hair up like always, they let it down, just attaching brands of her hair up.

"Marvelous," Daisy whispered in awe once they were done.

Arlette's lips found a smile. "Thank you."

"Oh! We almost forgot!" One of the maids exclaimed, going through something eagerly, then after many noises, humming in relief.

"How did I forget about the mask," Daisy's unique voice says in disbelief.

"Mask?" Arlette was surprised. She didn't know she had to wear a mask.

"Yeah," Daisy answered. "Everybody is to wear one,"

Interesting, Arlette thought. She liked the idea of it.

They placed the mask on her face.

It felt strange—it covered from the middle of her nose and up over her eyebrows. She'd never worn a mask. Her sisters told her most of them were lovely and foreign, with beautiful designs. It was like one more piece of jewelry.

Arlette's fingers found her upper cheekbone, which was covered in the mask. She moved her fingers over the strange material. It indeed had many designs and shapes and different textures. She liked how different it felt to the familiar texture of the dresses or actual jewelry.

"I like it," Arlette said, smiling.

Daisy laughed lightly. "You're ready now, miss. You must go, the Prince is waiting downstairs."

Her heart accelerated at the mention of him. He was waiting for her. Arlette didn't know how to feel about that. She always felt something when it came to him. Whether it was fear, panic, nerves, or longing, or anything that made her heart hammer erratically on her chest.

Daisy guided her out of the room and to the top of the stairs, where she told Arlette good bye and wished she enjoys her night. She could hear the soft music playing downstairs. Arlette nodded, starting to get nervous, hugging her, and saying goodbye. Before Daisy left though, she whispered in her ear, "It'll be okay, miss, I promise."

Arlette nodded once again, swallowing when Daisy let her go.

Arlette walked down the stairs, the light melody engulfing her ears. She could also hear people chatting and glasses clicking. As she neared the bottom, she instantly knew the Prince was right down there waiting. His presence penetrated her whole being and filled her veins with something she couldn't describe.

She came to the bottom, unfamiliar as to where to go. But the Prince took her hand, startling Arlette for a moment. His emotions quickly hit Arlette, though they were unknown, clouded, mixed, and all over the place. All at once, like always. It always took Arlette a moment to try to identify one of them.

He ran his thumb over her knuckles. "You look beautiful,"

Those simple words made something inside her bloom with strong, triggering emotions. She felt her face get warm and her fingers prinkly. "Thank you,"

His scent was overwhelming, yet Arlette liked it.

"My condolences to you and your family," the Prince said, making Arlette's head pick up and following his taunting voice.

Arlette couldn't find the words to answer, but if she had, she would've probably broken down. And she didn't the think the Prince was expecting a response from her silence. Maybe he understood.

Once they'd stepped into the large, spacious place with people all over the place laughing and talking, he asked her to dance once the next song started playing, and Arlette couldn't bring herself to deny. She'd always liked to dance.

The Prince took her to what she felt the center of big room, placing his strong hand on her lower back. Arlette tensed, but placed her hand on his shoulder with ease. Right away, they were moving to the rhythm of the delightful and powerful music. The Prince moved her effortlessly, periodically pushing her closer to his body. Arlette had gasped but quickly, he extended his arm, making her twirled. She smiled. His lips were close to her ear, she could feel his soft breath.

Arlette turned, twirled, and spun in his arms. She had poured herself out dancing with him. And he was magnificent. He knew how to handle women—that was the only thing Arlette concluded, and he did it well. The music was intense, passionate, intimate, like it was made only for the two of them. She felt like she was in a dream. Arlette came closer to his body and arched her back on his arm. She felt him come closer to her body as she went back up slowly.

The music was over.

He was so close to her that she could feel the quick breaths he catched. She could feel his piercing gaze on her and Arlette felt as if she was on fire. She felt a pure and powerful feeling shake her up. His scent was wrapping around her like a haunting snake. And for a moment, she longed for his lips on hers and for his arms around her. She craved for the same thing she felt when he'd last kissed her. That so, so captivating, mesmerizing, and deadly feeling, where she felt like she was going to explode and disappear. She wanted to feel once more how his lips felt around hers, how he wrapped his hands around her body, how she felt lov—

Everyone started to clap joyously, making Arlette come back to reality, making slightly pull back.

Bur far, far away she could hear a familiar voice, whispering, Such a pity you're in love with a monster...

The voice sounded disgusted, disappointed and it made the hairs from Arlette's back rise.

That voice was that woman's voice from Arlette's dream.

"My lady! You look beautiful tonight," someone complimented and Arlette gave a small smile, thanking the lady.

Arlette rested her hand beside the Prince's elbow as he guided her.

After that, all the queens and princesses and people from other lands came to Arlette, all intrigued to know about her. Arlette introduced herself to all of them, smiling politely from time to time.

"You're so beautiful!"

"I've never seen hair like yours, my lady, breathtaking!"

"Wow, your family is blessed to have you, miss."

Arlette was so overwhelmed by their joy and questions and compliments. The Prince hadn't said a word and Arlette was starting to worry. She didn't know why, but she was.

Another song started playing and he took her again to dance, but this time, without warning. She didn't mind though. She was just itching with curiosity to know what was on his mind.

The song was softer than the previous one.

Arlette placed her hand on his shoulder again, only this time, much closer to his neck, while he placed his hand on her lower back. And she rested her head on his chest. They moved smoothly to the rhythm of the music. Arlette was feeling brave, so she took the opportunity. "What's...wrong, Your Highness?" Though she didn't move to look up at him.

"Vince," he said in her ear. "Call me Vince."

Vince...

Arlette picked up her head, following his voice.

"Vince..." she whispered to herself, tasting the name in her tongue.

"Perfect," he whispered, then went back to her question. "My father's behavior is worrying me."

Arlette's eyebrows rose. "What is he doing?"

"Drinking,"

Arlette pursed her lips. For some reason, she already knew he was drowning his sorrows in drinks.

She could hear the Prince's concern in his voice even though he didn't want to admit it.

Arlette couldn't hold it back anymore, her hands felt like they were going to explode. They screeched, eager touch him. Slowly, Arlette moved the hand from his shoulder to his artistic neck, and then his cheekbone. It was partially covered in the mask he wore, but Arlette could feel as he slightly tensed under her touch. The intensity she felt by touching him was driving her mad. She could feel the ferocity of it, making her want to touch his whole body. What was hidden under all those clothes, all the art sculptured in his body. She moved her hand to his jawline, feeling the fascinating art embedded and carved in his skin. Arlette could never get enough of it.

"He'll be alright," she said quietly, smiling softly up at him. Arlette knew that sometimes life hit people with things they had no control over. And people coped with it in many different ways.

The music came to an end.

"Arlette...? Arlette!"

Her head snapped toward the voice. "Ember?" she gradually pulled away from the Prince, slowly following where she last heard her sister.

"Arlette! Lords..." Ember embraced her sister in long, warm hug. "I've been looking for you the whole night. Lords, this place is huge."

Arlette pulled away. "Why? What's wrong?"

Ember suddenly hesitated, "N-nothing. We just have to talk,"

Arlette turned around, where she felt the Prince's ravishing eyes on her. She tried to form out the words...but couldn't. Hopefully, her sister stepped in. "May I have a word with my sister, Your Highness?" Her voice was flat and cold and it surprised Arlette.

The Prince didn't say a word, but Arlette figured he probably accepted because quickly, Ember took Arlette another way, dragging further and further away from the Prince.

Ember stopped, and Arlette could feel the cold breeze of the night bite at her flesh and hear the trees rustle in the distance. They were in a balcony.

Arlette was starting to worry as she hugged herself from the cold. "Tell me what's wrong Ember,"

Ember took a deep breath. "Mom told me something I was in denial of, and I had to see it myself."

Arlette frowned, curious. "And what is that?"

"You." she started. "That you were going to end up falling in love with the beast,"

"Ember I—"

"I saw how you first danced with him. Your eyes were glowing and your hair was radiant. You touched him like nobody else could. And I swear, Arlette, it was like you could see him, like there was no one else in the world but him. You love him."

Arlette was in utter shock, she'd been lost of words, like she'd always been lately. But this left her mind in blank.

"You don't have to tell me anything, but mom said you have damned us all," There was a silence.

Arlette felt a pang in her heart, reminding her, "It was Fate,"

"Yes, it was Fate indeed, but maybe it wasn't the best decision she made,"

Arlette took her sister's hand in hers, "Ember, you don't understand. It's something I can't control. I didn't even know I—"

Ember yanked her hand away from her sister's grip, furious. "How could you? I thought you were going to fight off the pull, but you didn't! This was supposed to be temporary! Father would've worked, gotten the money we needed, and we'd be gone, and the pull would've lessened!"

Arlette was hurt. "You yourself said I couldn't fight it off! I tried telling you to escape, but you wouldn't have it." She was furious, adding, "You make it seem so easy, I tried everything I could to fight it off, to forget about it and about him, but I couldn't. You don't understand and you never will!"

"I told you that because I thought you were already fighting off! It was the beginning of the bond, so it could've easily be broken. But now..." Ember trailed, quite disappointed.

Those strong feelings and thoughts Arlette was having were part of the bond. Those elusive things she couldn't put her finger on—couldn't understand. The ferocious pull and longing that tugged at her heart and soul...it was all part of it and she didn't even noticed.

Arlette shook her head. "You are making no sense, Ember. Even if I tried you know I couldn't. It was inevitable."

Ember ignored her. "Mother has been exploring your abilities, you know ..."

"I do," Arlette answered.

"Good. At least you know you're evil,"

Arlette was shocked, she opened her mouth to talk but was cut off by someone else.

"Arlette...wow, you look marvelous tonight."

Arlette turned her head towards the voice. It was Aaron.

Arlette heard his footsteps as he neared her. Once her was near enough, he grabbed her hand, kissing it softly.

"Hello, Aaron," she greeted quietly, surprisingly glad he was there.

"It's been quite a time since I last saw you," he said, then greeted Ember as well, who was quiet the whole time, before she excused herself, leaving Arlette with Aaron.

As soon as Ember disappeared, Aaron had embraced Arlette, taking her by surprise. "I've missed you so much," he whispered in her ear, breathing her in.

"I missed you too," Arlette replied, though somehow eager to pull away from him.

Finally, he pulled away, resting his hand on Arlette's hip and caressing her cheekbone. In the process, he slid away her mask.

Arlette didn't want to tell him how uncomfortable she was under his touch, instead, she smiled. "How have you been?"

"Horrible,"

There was something different about Aaron. He was eager, his personality blunt and strange. Arlette wondered what caused him to be like he was right now.

"Not being able to see you was driving me crazy," he said seriously, though laughing humorlessly at the end.

Regardless, Arlette gave him a small smile. "Everything just went out of control the last time I'd met with you," Arlette remembered out-loud.

Aaron suddenly pulled her roughly closer to his body, making her gasp. "Yeah, but now you're here and no one can take you away from me,"

She tried to pull away softly, "Aaron I-I—"

"Shh..." he hushed, his breath brushing Arlette's lips.

She struggled away under his dead grip. "Aaron...you're hurting me,"

He chuckled. "Oh, am I?" Arlette's eyes filled with tears as she was being pushed roughly against a wall. She felt all her breath disappear when her back hit the wall.

Arlette pushed back the tears. "Aar-Aaron please..."

His hand was on the side of her neck and cheek and the other one was grabbing forcibly her hip. "Please what, my dear?" He asked, his face on her neck.

Arlette swallowed. "Let me g-go,"

He breathed her in, then moved his face from her neck, "That won't be possible, darling."

Arlette could feel his eyes boring holes into her soul, making her feel bare and naked under them.

"Your lips...I've always wanted to kiss them," He whispered, grabbing her face and slamming his lips against hers.

Arlette felt disgusted and violated. No one had ever man-handled her like Aaron had. The last person she'd expected to do that was him. It made her heart ripped into shreds. But she didn't respond to the lips moving around hers. They felt wrong and vile. He noticed right away because he slammed her once again against the wall, kissing her once again. Arlette fought under his sickening grip, trying to push him away from her. When he pulled away from the kiss, she screamed louder than she ever could, begging for help. Aaron covered her mouth, chuckling.

"No one's here to save you, darling,"

---

a/n: Wow, wow, wow. I've updated in less than a week! I think I should get an award for that. PLUS, it's a pretty long chapter, so even more reason to get an award, LOL. No, I'm just kidding, hahaha. I was just so excited to write this chapter, once I started I couldn't stop (it was actually going to be longer but I was like eh no).

Anyways, I apologize for any mistakes, this is not entirely edited.

p.s COMMENT AND VOTE AND COMMENT I want to hear all your thoughts about this chapter!

- nessie xoxo

Blind Beauty | 21

To not overwhelm you I tried to keep this, you know...somewhat appropriate.

Credits to Living_for_Death for the great banner on the side!

Chapter Veintiuno

Beast's P.O.V.

When he'd first seen her, he was left without words, and that rarely ever happened.

She looked beyond enthralling. Her beauty and innocence absorbed and thrashed his whole being, captivating and setting his attention only on her. Her touch had rubbed his corrupted bones in a way that he'd never experienced before and he craved it even more after she'd pull her hand away. The thick, twisted veins that traveled his body pumped ferociously, trying to tell him something. She was like a goddess; powerful though calm, like a sleeping dragon. He could stare at her all night if he could.

He was somewhat shocked when she danced with him. Her hair glowed strongly and her eyes screamed unknown words to him. Everyone stared. People had asked questions about her hair but no one had explanation to it. And he didn't really mind. He liked how her hair glowed, like it was only for him to do that. It was fierce and intense and it spoke to him. Her scent was striking, compelling, and pure. It'd almost drove him to the edge of rebellion, but he composed himself. One could say he was almost proud from the many times he'd done that. But he wished he could see her whole face under that mask, every wild, eager, and emotional expression she'd often have. Her features were delicate and inviting and as always, he could look at them forever.

She had been gone for a while now and he was slowly starting to worry.

He'd even talked to his father, roughly getting some sense into him, which thankfully worked. But she still hadn't come back.

He decided to follow the direction he'd last seen her frame disappeared, walking through the mass and groups of people, his intense eyes looking for a certain figure.

He didn't see her anywhere.

Guardians suggested to accompany him, but he dismissed them.

Figuring her sister probably wanted some privacy, he went further into the empty depths of the palace, where as he walked more and more, felt a cold breeze come and sway over him. He stopped and looked to the far left, where he could see a balcony, white curtain blowing with the breeze.

As silence strained in, distant sobs from the balcony echoed to him.

Just as he neared the balcony, he could see a trembling figure on the corner of the floor, rocking their bodies back and forth.

He moved the blowing curtain away from his view, stepping into the balcony and realizing who the figure sobbing on the floor was.

It was her.

His eyes widened and his soul exploded with a seething, bleeding anger, asking himself who dared to break her like this.

She looked up, her eyes twinkling and drowned in tears with a thousand emotions, mask no longer on her face, sobbing out the words, "I-I'm so s-sorry...I-I didn't m-mean to d-do it..." She sniffled as merciless tears fell down her face. "I-I was just d-defending myself..."

He didn't quite understand what she was talking about until he looked down to his left, where his brother's body was laying on the floor. Aaron's face was smashed with deep bruises and cuts. His lips had been severely bitten and his right arm was abnormally twisted over his head and behind his back, clothes awfully wrinkled. It was like a wolf had attacked him.

She...did that to him? He could only wonder. Looking at her then at Aaron and back again, he had no words as he ran his hand through his neatly combed hair.

Aaron suddenly made a soft grunting noise, making him come back his senses. He quickly called for the guardians to take care of Aaron and with ease, went for his beauty, taking her in his arms and walking away from the shocked guardians.

□   □   □   □   □   □

Arlette's P.O.V.

She didn't know where all that strength came from. Arlette had just realized one of her hands was free when Aaron had his hand over her mouth, and she just took that opportunity to...

Arlette shook her head, trying to forget her vicious act. True, she was defending herself, but that didn't justify the way she struck Aaron on the face constantly, like she had no control over what she was doing. She'd also slammed him against the wall in the hallway then drag him back into the balcony... all without laying a finger on him. When his body collided with the wall, Arlette could hear the wall crack, making the whole place shake.

She wondered if the Prince noticed it.

But Arlette regretted it—she had gone a little bit too far. Way too far. Yet, that didn't seem to bother the Prince.

Now she was here, in his room, on his bed, pondering over the argument that she and Ember had. And he was at the door, talking with a few guardians about what happened to Aaron.

Ember had blamed Arlette for everything. From not "fighting off" the pull, to their father's death. Arlette felt betrayed and truthfully, guilty. Maybe it was her fault all of this happened. But what could she have done? Nothing, really. Arlette did her best for everything to go smoothly, she followed her mom's and grandma's wishes of not doing something she'd regret—well most of the time, and had, in her knowledge, behaved. Still, nothing really justified how Ember accused her for everything that turned their lives upside down—that ended her father's life. It just didn't make sense to Arlette. Had her mom gotten into Ember's head trying to convince her or something? Arlette didn't know. She could only wonder.

The door closed, bringing Arlette out of her thoughts. She could feel the Prince slowly approach her and Arlette wondered if Aaron was dead or not.

"He's alive," he said, as if reading her thoughts.

Arlette exhaled, relieved or scared, she didn't know, and shivered as she felt his presence come near her.

By instinct, she quickly stood up from the bed, suddenly colliding against his body.

In no time, his arm was around her waist, making Arlette gasp.

Arlette didn't know he'd been that close to her. But she didn't pull away, neither did he.

The air around them shifted slowly but surely. Arlette could feel her heart hammering crazily on her chest and her senses began clouding with an overwhelming feeling. As bad as her thoughts and the situation was, she didn't want this moment to stop.

She could feel the way he breathed in and out. Steadily, precisely, even though his body was tense against hers.

Arlette wanted to let him know that he shouldn't feel like that when she was near him, so, to break the tension, she smiled softly up at him, bringing her hand up his cheek. He didn't have his mask on anymore, which she was thankful for. The artwork graved on his face was, as always, enticing and painfully fascinating, making Arlette long for more.

She was taken aback when a growl escaped his lips. It was low and unpredictable. And everything just happened so fast after that. Before she knew it, Arlette was being thrown on the bed with an inexplicable force, but bounced on it comfortably. In not time, his warm body was on top of hers.

Arlette had her hands on either side of his shoulders, gasping for breath from the utter shock as he breathed her in, an intense, violent feeling crawling up her whole body.

She could hear screeching, tormented screams as his warm, mystifying lips travelled her neck, leaving a fiery sensation in his path. Arlette's sharp intakes of breath were a clue that she was trying not explode into a million fragments under him. She'd never experienced anything like this.

Flowingly, Arlette found his hair. It was long and lots, almost able to put into a low, short ponytail. She digged her fingers in, feeling his soft, loose curls as he kissed her collarbones.

His lips on her skin felt bizarre in the most breathtaking way.

It was like Arlette could feel his inner monster.

He picked up his head, his lips a string away from touching hers, and he didn't move. He stayed that way for the longest of seconds, probably minutes. It was almost painful for Arlette. As much as she wanted to deny it, she insanely craved for his lips on hers.

It was like he was waiting for her to say something.

Silence strained in.

"Kiss me, Vince," she whispered, liking how his name rolled off her tongue. Her soft voice seeming to echo through the whole room.

Almost instantly, his ravishing lips were on hers with a new hunger.

The Prince's lips were warm and chaotic and blissful all at once. Arlette kissed him with wildness and fire. And once again, she found her hand in his unruly hair, longing for more. Her lips ran ardently over his, desire present in both of them. Arlette could hear the low growls escaping his lips and the passion between them boiled. This was like an obscure, electrifying, and deep feeling that struck them both with temper, and Arlette loved it. She'd never felt this way with anybody. No strong feeling or emotion could compare to this severely explosive, craving, and intoxicating feel.

This made her see things in a whole new perspective.

He suddenly pulled away, his breathing hard.

Arlette could feel her heart wanting to come out of her rib cage as she ran a hand over his chest, down to his stomach, involuntarily wondering for what might be under.

Suddenly, she heard a low growl from him, while clothes ripped into shreds, the sound resonating through the whole room.

She had a pretty good idea of what it was.

As if by instinct, her hand flew to his bare torso.

Immediately, Arlette was captivated. Her hands ran ever so carefully over his complex, alluring torso, touching the long wisps of...his skin, but they felt more like very, very thick veins. They were baffling and riveting, caging her fascination like a bird. There was movement underneath, like there was something running underneath them, and they throbbed, just the slightest bit. Arlette used both of her hands, grasping every bit of it. How thick they were at the bottom of his stomach, then went up to his collarbones, becoming slimmer—it was like someone had embedded art on him, like his body, just like his face, was a canvas.

His emotions were constantly changing under her touch, but suddenly, Arlette could feel regret and pain stab her like a knife in her chest.

He quickly pulled away from her, getting off of her.

Arlette felt a pang in her heart, leaving her with an empty, dreadful feel. Surprised, she supported her upper weight on her elbows, shifting slowly into a sitting position. She felt her face flushed and hot all over but she didn't mind.

Arlette could feel his weight dawning at the edge of the bed so, carefully, attentively, she kneeled on the bed, getting near him. Long seconds later, as if afraid of his reaction, she placed her hand on his shoulder. And involuntarily, her hand ran over his toned back, not placing it back on his shoulder, but instead taking both of her arms around his neck. He flinched the slightest bit under her touch.

She brought her lips to his ear. "What's wrong?"

There was a long, prickly silence.

"I'm a monster,"

He said it with disgust and hatred, with a poisonous, cold voice, like she should be horrified and grossed for kissing him or even touching him. Like he didn't deserve any of her closeness and desire—as if he was only doomed to inflict fear and terror. Like he was doomed to be in isolation for the rest of his days.

But he didn't treat her as if he was a monster - not anymore. And to her, he wasn't one.

She turned his face to hers, shaking her head. "You're not," she smiled. "And if you are, then you're my monster." To her, he was a man . . . and a beast—a handsome beast. He was art and he was beautiful and enrapturing in the most dangerous, electrifying way.

Arlette felt something inside of him thrash.

With an unbelievable speed, she was once again fired on the bed, his lips crashing against hers with a new, fathomless desire.

He caressed her cheek, intoxicating her with fervor, running his hands down her neck and to the her dress.

Pausing, he tenderly slipped the the thin straps off her shoulder, his careful touch scratching the walls of her sanity.

Arlette knew where this was going and truthfully, she didn't want it to stop. She had already made up her made when Ember, and everyone else, showed their true colors. Also, her feelings toward him couldn't be any more undeniable, even the woman from her dreams knew. But she knew everything, didn't she?

He slid her dress off her body slowly, with tenderness. Arlette had to admit, she was severely nervous and somewhat scared. Feeling her face, neck and chest become hot with overwhelmness, her mind screeched. But he treated her so carefully, as if she was going to shatter into a million pieces any moment, and Arlette felt that there was no better other moment than this one.

Arlette knew what people did behind closed doors, or at least she had an idea. Her sisters were very detailed at explaining their experiences with men. They advised Arlette heavily on what she should do if she was in this situation.

Maybe she should listen to them.

There was a long pause after he slid her dress off, and she, slowly, was starting to doubt his intentions.

Not before he said in dangerously low voice, "Beautiful,"

The sound of his voice washed over her, making her shiver.

The rest of the night was a pure, wild bliss.

It was perfect.

Arlette didn't need to follow her sisters' techniques or advice and ways when being with a man.

He made love to her slow and passionate at first, making tendrils of fire curl around her skin. She'd shivered and moaned as bolts of pure ecstasy pounded through her. He stroke her hair, proceeding to leave trails of steamy kisses along her body. He was so hot and masculine, so dark and deadly, his scent and presence poured on her like heavy rain, making her grab desperately for his shoulders.

But then, she was drowned in his luring fury. It became wild, hard, and ardent, making her arch her back and moan his name in ways she thought she never could, touching her in places that not even in her most dauntless dreams she thought someone could.

His touch left a burning trail of fire along her skin that made her only want him, only want the Prince, only Vince as powerful and bad as he was. He'd pounded inside of her with intense rage and craving, her screams for more only intensifying. It was like they couldn't get enough of each other. She could feel that through their passion, their bond became even more enduring, stronger, piercing both of their souls in the most inflamed, violent way possible.

No one would'd believed this, but Arlette was something close to being tragically, fatally, and undeniably in love with the Beast.

---

a/n: I know you guys are probably like WHUUUUUT, but comment anyways because I'm not really that happy with this chapter even though it took me forever and a day to write. I know I haven't revealed why Aaron acted the way he did, but I promise...soon, most likely in the next chapter. I'm slow guys, I apologize, lol. But anyway, the remaining contents of this chapter is left to your imagination. ;) hahaha. Also,

this is not edited entirely.

p.s I miss the banners on the side.

- nessie xoxo

M ADE SOMETHING---------->

Chapter Veintidós

A sense of nausea filled Arlette's stomach, clotting it. She didn't know whether to feel glad or terrified that the evil woman wasn't the one talking to her. Instead, it was Ember.

Ember. Who had drastically and painfully changed.

"You...you damned yourself!" Ember accused, her footsteps quickly gaining speed toward Arlette. Arlette backed away frighteningly as she spoke. "And all of us!"

Once close enough, Ember pushed her hard, making her slam against a wall.

"How?" Arlette screamed. "How? How? How?" Tears streamed down her face as confusion and desperation clung to her soul.

Ember stabbed Arlette with her finger on her chest repeatedly as she spat out the answer. "You know really well how! Everything that has happened...it's your fault! Mother was right. Your powers do come from evil, and evil always brings bad stuff upon lives."

Ember's words stabbed at her heart, making everything crumble within her, but also making anger start to snare up her chest.

"Father said I wasn't—"

"Oh father, our dear father..." Ember drawled mockingly. "He doesn't—didn't know anything about your powers—"

"Shut up!" Arlette had had it with her sister. Furious, she started walking, making her sister back away. "I, for the hundredth time, don't come from evil. Why are you and mom so dead set on that? What have I done? All my life, all I've ever seen is darkness. Darkness and nothing else. Aren't these abilities some kind of...gift? Power?"

"You don't understand, Arlette. You are a descendant of that man! That horrible man Griselda married—"

"So are you, Ember—"

"But you're just like him. Mom told me that. You're just like him, though you still haven't developed all your powers."

But Arlette didn't feel like she was this wicked, frightening being. She didn't feel the need to kill or destroy. On the contrary, she repelled the thought of killing someone. So why was Ember so convinced that whatever Arlette was wasn't good?

"You're making no sense, Ember." Arlette said to her sister.

"Not now, but soon…" Ember promised.

Arlette shook her head, reminding herself, "This is just a dream,"

"It is indeed. But what's about to happen won't be,"

Arlette sucked in a sharp breath through her mouth, her spine arching with the effort. Then her body shook awake bluntly, making her shoot up on the bed.

Her heart hammered against her chest with force, making her breathe heavily. She was awake. It was just a dream—a nightmare. Just a nightmare, she reminded herself.

"Thank the Lord, you're finally awake,"

It was Daisy.

Arlette frowned.

But before she could respond, as if by instinct, Arlette ran her hand on the mattress beside her, her heart clenching. He wasn't there…he left. Instead, in his place, there were the soft blankets, all sprawled around her. And his scent, his masculine, dark, addictive scent.

Suddenly, everything that happened the night before came crashing upon her with force. The Ball. The Prince. Cold argument with Ember. A bleeding Aaron. The Prince… Oh yes. She did remember. She remembered everything. Especially last night with the Prince. Arlette had been reckless, most accordingly to her family, for doing what she did, but she didn't regret it. She had gone to heaven and come back.

Yes, she didn't deny that due to it being her first time, there was pain. But that pain didn't compare to what he made her feel. She had been drowned into an abyss she couldn't escape even if she wanted to. An abyss of passion. Rapture. Ecstasy. Euphoria.

Something dropped, disturbing Arlette's thoughts.

She didn't realize she was butt naked until she felt a chilly breeze smack her exposed breasts, causing her to rapidly take a blanket and put it on her chest.

"What are you doing here?" Arlette asked in confusion, grabbing the blanket and putting it all around her, like a towel, before getting to her feet. She felt slightly sore down there but she didn't mind.

Daisy sighed. She was somewhere in the room, probably picking up whatever fell. "Sewin'. The Prince ordered for me to look after you 'til you wake up," she said calmly. "He...had an emergency and gave me strict orders not to wake you,"

"How long have you been here?" Arlette had a feeling Daisy had been here for a while.

"Couple of fine hours," She answered, walking towards Arlette.

Before Arlette could ask the time, Daisy told her, "It's a quarter to four,"

Her eyes widened. "What?"

"Yeah…I was beginnin' to think you were a lil' dead when I tried to wake you but you wouldn't wake up for Lord's sake," Daisy stood in front of Arlette, her soft lavender scent brushing over her nose. She sounded quite desperate, briefly recalling.

Arlette gave her a small smile, feeling mildly guilty for almost giving Daisy a heart attack.

"…I was dreaming,"

"Thank God," she sounded relieved, quickly coming closer to Arlettte and changing the topic as she took one red strand from Arlette's hair and twirled it around her fingers. "From what I can see, miss, you indeed enjoyed your night," she giggled innocently.

Arlette's cheeks reddened immediately. "I—"

"Don't worry, I won't tell. You have my word."

Arlette smiled at her, nodding her head. "Thank you,"

"Where is he?" Arlette couldn't control herself. She had tried not to ask and seem noisy, but the curiosity and something more was just killing her.

Daisy seemed to hesitate the slightest bit before answering. "He..." she started, then paused, sighing. "Nobody knows, really. He took off looking troubled this morning. He hasn't come back ever since. The King has been looking for him because they need to talk but he's nowhere to be seen."

Should that have made Arlette feel worried? Concerned? Because she was. And that frightened her. She shouldn't. She shouldn't have had this thick, sick, twisted sensation prickling all over her skin, alarming all of her senses, telling her something wasn't right. At all. There were whispers, those familiar whispers she seemed to strangely miss. They said inaudible babbles, becoming louder and louder as her stomach churned.

Something's not right.

Something's not right.

Go. Go! You need to go!

"Miss?"

But the voices kept whispering. They had never whispered as clearly and as painfully eager as now.

Time is ticking.

Must go. Must go.

"Arlette? What's wrong?" Daisy sounded worried, her voice rising to a squeaky tone.

"...I...I need to go..."

"Go? Go where?"

He will die.

He will die!

"The Dark Forest,"

"What?" Daisy shrieked. "Are you crazy? If you go to the Dark Forest you will perish. Your soul will be there. Trapped and lost. You know that, Arlette."

She knew. She just wanted—needed to go.

Now.

"Hand me some clothes, Daisy. Simple, please." Arlette didn't have time to argue. She needed to go.

Daisy sighed, her breath coming out shaky. "Arlette, please—"

"I'm serious, Daisy. This is serious."

"B-but what are you going to do over there? Just wait for the Prince. There's nothing there...other than torment and death—"

Arlette didn't want to tell her the reason why. She knew Daisy will freak out. Instead she said, "Come with me. You'll stay outside while I go in. I will be fine. I promise." Arlette said surely, though she didn't really know if she was going to be okay. There was no certainty on that. She could die in a matter of minutes for all she knew. "I will try to come out before it settles on me,"

"...You're crazy...this is crazy. How—" Daisy cut herself off, not grasping the fact that Arlette wanted to go willingly inside the Dark Forest. "...Are you sure? This—"

"Positive. Now, can you please hand me some comfortable clothes?" Time was ticking and Arlette was still here. Not a good sign.

Daisy finally skittered out of the room, quickly returning with trousers and a blouse.

Arlette wasn't really acquaintanced with these clothes—she had only wore dresses all her life.

"This is mine actually. Your closet is full of dresses - dresses that will just be a burden if you plan to enter..." Daisy didn't even want to mention it. She cleared her throat. "My father got the trousers from the outside world when he went to explore it. Anyways, the blouse—"

Arlette quickly yanked Daisy's clothes from her hands, "Thank you, Daisy." She dropped the blanket, slipping in her undergarments, then the blouse, quickly throwing it over her head. When she got to the trousers, though, she was having quite some trouble.

"Here, let me help you," Daisy suggested, taking the trousers from her hands and slipping them on Arlette.

Soon enough, the two of them were running from the back of the palace, too afraid to grab a horse and increase the chances of getting caught. Arlette was sweating from the nauseous nerves and Daisy was beyond paranoic and twitchy. Every time she urged Arlette on, it was like she felt sick.

They were both wearing a cloak after Daisy's constant pepperings and complaints about Arlette's hair being too under someone's nose and obvious. But Arlette was glad—it was getting very cold.

"Wait..." Arlette panted. "I need to breathe," her lungs ached and her feet throbbed for running non stop.

Daisy finally stopped. "Yeah, I think we should be fine from now on. No one will see us," she said breathless. "But we have to hurry, the sun will set soon,"

Arlette caught up to her and then they started walking at a decent pace, stepping into dirt and mud, bushes, and leafs.

A forest.

Two ladies alone in a forest was not something you saw everyday—it was risky and unsafe, but this was no ordinary trip. Every time they walked deeper and deeper into this sparse forest, the voices in her mind screeched tormented and thorny screams, telling—warning her that she was getting closer and closer. Arlette had a bad, bad sensation biting into her skin deep into her bones. She had never, ever felt this acrid, bitter, and cruel feeling in her being telling her that something was just not right. The whispers never made out clear words, they were always inaudible babbles and mutters. Not until now. They were still whispers, but clearer and blunt.

"Lord Aaron wanted to see you,"

Arlette ripped herself out of her thoughts at this, the cold wind biting into the features of her face.

"He wanted to see me?" She couldn't believe this. First, he had the audacity of disrespecting her in the most vile way possible and now he wanted to see her after he was almost beaten to death by her for that?

Arlette could've laughed.

"He begged for me to wake you but I wouldn't. I'd already had orders from the Prince not to." She paused. "He said he wanted to apologize for what he did last night—that he didn't know what came over him,"

Arlette shook her head disbelievingly. How could he be sorry? Perhaps he didn't mean to...? Why was he trying to apologize? He did mean it. Arlette told herself. The way he grabbed her...talked to her. It was all too real, too harsh. Arlette shuddered from the memory. No one had ever treated like that. Like she was...nothing.

"I don't know what he did that had him look so devastated, but whatever it is, Arlette, I think you need to talk to him about it at some point," Daisy said honestly and Arlette could hear as she stepped on a branch. Hard.

"What else did he tell you?"

"Nothin'." Daisy said simply. "But I saw your sister too."

Her head snapped towards Daisy. "Who? Ember?"

"No, the other one—Cary—Cou—Camy—"

"Cade." Arlette corrected.

"Yeah, her…" Daisy said in a weird tone. "Is she always lost in space? Like she's in her own little world?"

Arlette shrugged. "I guess."

"Oh I think yes." Daisy inquired, convinced. "Do you know she always wanders off to the forest? It's like she has a secret lover or something,"

"Perhaps." Arlette said, hearing birds overhead.

"But why would she keep it a secret?"

"She...tends to like older men—married men," Arlette clarified.

"Oh...well, that's no good. She can easily be broken. Some men are just too cruel."

Arlette shrugged once again, wondering why suddenly they were talking about Cade's secret love life. But she didn't mind as long as that sick, sinking feeling in her stomach would stop. "She says younger men don't fill her soul like older men do. Says that most young men are boring and innocent. She likes the... thrill and danger that comes with someone forbidden and experienced." As soon as those words escaped her lips, she felt like she had said too much. She always did. But either she said too little or too much.

Funny how her sisters told Arlette all their secrets but at the same time became distant in the most strangest of ways.

Daisy was quiet for a moment, making Arlette's stomach churn as she walked past a thorny bush. "Ha, she's a lil' rebel." Daisy finally said. "Envious of her bravery though. Married men?" Daisy asked incredulously but at the same time almost admiring. "In the village that I grew up in, if any woman had their hands where they shouldn't, best believe she won't last a night with 'em."

Arlette didn't answer right away but when she was, Daisy came to an abrupt halt.

Arlette frowned, stopping. "What's wrong?"

She could hear Daisy swallow as she muttered, "Oh precious Fate, protect us from what we fear most...forgive us for walking to our own death..."

Arlette could feel a vile lump in throat, her hands suddenly trembling.

Then Daisy turned to Arlette.

"We're here."

Arlette's heart pounded on her chest with force, the whispers in her head increasing in speed. They were abnormally and feverishly fast, frightening and twisting Arlette. She swallowed, praying to Fate for protection.

Arlette gave two steps forward, the trees overhead rustling and the Dark Forest luring her in.

"Wait." Daisy called, grabbing her hand, making Arlette turn around.

"Be careful and please don't die," Daisy said quietly. "Whatever you are going to do, do it fast before it settles on you. Follow the path—you'll feel it."

Arlette nodded gingerly, sensing fear come from Daisy in strong waves.

"Just scream if anything, okay?" Daisy said almost miserably. "I'll call for help,"

But they both knew they were too far away to get help anywhere near. Nobody lived close to a place like this. Regardless, Arlette nodded once again, saying, "I promise,"

At last, Daisy let go of her hand and Arlette slowly turned around, starting to walk several steps before she felt lured in by the Dark Forest.

As she walked deeper into the forest, she felt like it was shrinking, closing down on her. She could no longer hear the chirping of the birds or the dying sun on her skin. The forest was cold, eerie. Blood-curdling shutters rocked down her spine. The ground beneath her was hard, it didn't feel like she was walking on dirt and for some sick reason, that frightened her. Arlette could hear sinister noises from afar, as if by every step she took, she was awakening something lethal, merciless.

Soon, she wondered why the whispers send her here. But the need to come here was killing her—it was enough. She knew he was here. She could feel it.

Arlette could feel his pain. He was pained and in agony and furious, making her heart clench and her soul tear apart. Arlette's thoughts started to fill with questions. What was happening to him? Did someone bring him here? Did he seek death? Her soul crushed at the many possibilities.

She could feel, and almost, hear him call to her, like he was too far away from reaching her. As if she was helplessly slipping between his fingers like sand.

Arlette walked faster, almost running, tears stinging her eyes as she feared the worst.

But soon, bumping hard against...someone.

Someone? In the Dark Forest?

Arlette took a few steps back.

"Arlette! My dear, how lovely to see you. I was waiting for your arrival."

Oh no.

It was her. The evil woman from her dreams—or nightmares.

But Arlette wasn't dreaming, she couldn't have been. "Wh-What—"

"Yes, my dear, I am real," she laughed in a vomiting sweet voice. "And so it's all of this...Still wondering why the forest hasn't settled on you though." she said in a tone laced with curiosity and amusement. "Looks like you don't have any fears. Hmm, you're quite something."

"I-I don't understand..." Why was this woman here? Why did she feel like she was at the wrong place at the wrong time? Why did she feel like whatever and everything that was happening was all tied down to this terrifying woman standing in front of her?

But she knew the answers to all those questions and she did understand, even if she didn't want to.

"Oh my sweet Arlette. Your beast is dying and look where you are. He's here but his fear won't let him reach you. His time is almost over," she sounded excited, and Arlette realized that this was like a game to her. A game her ill, twisted mind created.

"Where is he?" Arlette asked through gritted teeth as she tried to walk past her, her soul weeping to find him.

"Woah, now darlin', let's take this slow and chat for a bit," the woman said in a deadly, smooth voice as she grabbed Arlette by the arm.

She quickly yanked her hand away from her. "I don't have time—"

"I can't believe you gave yourself to him, dear." She laughed, but she said it in an admirable tone. "O' the innocent and sweet Arlette isn't so pure and innocent after all,"

Arlette's skin prickled. "How can you possibly—"

"I can't deny though, he really is good in bed..."

"Who are you?!" Arlette screamed, furious, frustrated, sad, exhausted, hurt, and everything else someone could possibly be. Her voice echoed through the eerie forest, and she felt something else awake from far away.

The woman laughed her usual obnoxious, sick laugh. Finally saying, "If you so insist, I am Simone, my dear. Witch of the witches and Lady of the Darkness. I was Vince's lover once—a long time ago as I told you. I made him what he is now; a cold, ruthless monster." She said in a smooth tone. Arlette suddenly remembered the story her mother told her about the Prince. It was...true. All of it. Arlette had been so foolish. "You want to know more, sugar? I was the one to destroy your village. I was the one who attacked your pretty little mind that night you were with Aaron. I was also the one who casted a spell on Aaron last night because I was bored and wanted to see pain, suffering, and tears." Her words seethed out cold and humorless. "I enjoy it,"

Arlette's eyes widened at all of this, fear and crumbling realization crashing down on her, making her step back several steps.

Voices screeched.

Everything clicked in place, like missing puzzle pieces appearing out of nowhere and finishing the picture.

Her eyes stung with tears.

There was just one last question she had and the only one that most mattered to her, "Did you..."

"No, my sweet Arlette." She said in a mocking tone. "I did not kill your father, your mother did."

Arlette went pale.

She could not believe this—wouldn't believe this.

Arlette felt her head spinning and her body become as light as a feather for a second with a clinging feeling in her stomach.

"She requested for one of my kind to kill your father. According to her, he was ruining her plans—of what? I don't know, but the crazy woman was literally desperate to get rid of him." Simone said this in a flat, bored tone. Like Arlette was just ruining the fun with all her questions.

Tears prickled at the edge of her orbs and she let them fall freely. How? How could her mother have done something like that? What drove her to the point where she no longer loved her husband and wanted to kill him? These things were peeling her sanity, really questioning anything and everything she has ever believed in—ever encountered. Her mother was against her. Arlette realized that all of this wasn't based just on a prediction. It was like her mother was blindly and deadly convinced that Arlette came from evil. Worse part was that something deep, deep inside Arlette told her that her mother wouldn't hesitate to get rid of her.

"Oh!" The woman suddenly exclaimed, coming back to sickly excited mood. "I forgot my gift dear, how rude of me,"

Arlette frowned, no longer deep in her thoughts. "Gift?"

"Yes, my dear. Your gift. I have yet to give it to you,"

"What is it?"

Simone chuckled, a wind suddenly picking up, blowing Arlette's hood off her head and making goosebumps rise up her arms. "The best gift someone could give you, of course."

Arlette didn't want a gift. She wanted to find him—find him and get him out of his agonizing misery and pain.

The tears streaming down her face wouldn't cease. "Just please, forget the gift. Tell me where he is."

"What you don't know is that he is so close, yet so far away. His fear is keeping you from finding him."

Arlette swallowed, a tingling sensation poking her body. "What's his fear?"

"Losing you," Simone said in a bitter tone. "Now your gift—"

Arlette ran. She didn't let her finish. Her footsteps padded harshly and rapidly on the ground, her whole body shaking with fear. She followed her instincts, desperately pushing and pushing through to hear him in her thoughts. Tears streamed down her face. "Vince!" Arlette screamed and sobbed his name at the top of her lungs, her voice resonating through the forest. Though she had a sinking feeling her gut, telling her that he was further away than she had thought. She tried to listen to his voice in her head, concentrating as she pushed through thorny, biting branches in her way.

Something else clogged up her mind though. Simone. Simone's laughter followed by her sour yet sweet voice in a foreign language before she said. "You will see the truth. The beast will soon be gone. Light will shatter your eyes, dear. You'll wish you never see it again."

---

a/n: NOT THE END. YET.

WILL BE EDITED SO KEEP AN EYE OUT.

LOVE YOU ALL,

- nessie xoxo

Blind Beauty | 23

PLEASE REFRESH IF YOU CANNOT SEE PAGE 2, 3, 4, 5, OR 6. THEY MAY APPEAR BLANK BUT THEY'RE NOT.

Chapter Veintitrés

Arlette could've had stayed at the palace—let things take their own accord. She could've had also fought the constant yanking in her soul telling her to go look for him. But she just couldn't. She couldn't let Fate do this to her. Not now. Yet Fate knew she would do this. She would look for him—look for him until she found him. And she didn't regret coming here. As crazy as it seemed, if she had to do this again, she would, without a thought. Because...because she couldn't let him die. She just couldn't.

Hearing Simone's voice, she felt thorns clinging to her body, every word she uttered out weighted by a dark, painful heaviness. She laughed and Arlette came to a halt. Arlette felt strange. Horribly strange. Not the fact that her body was feeling hot and cold and like she had pins studded all over her all at once, but the fact that the darkness she was used to seeing was not total darkness anymore. A faded light flickered across her vision. Her heart thumped madly, eagerly. What? Was it what she thought it was? But as soon as it came, it disappeared...and...and everything was just a blurry light. Arlette rubbed her eyes, feeling funny, and every time her hand ran over her eyes, the blurry lights and spots she was seeing were no longer blurry. Instead, she saw just about everything around her.

Arlette gasped in horror and astonishment. Just as described, the Dark Forest was indeed dark. Sculpted black and terrifying. Arlette rubbed her eyes feverishly once again, not believing what she was seeing. She blinked, letting her eyes run quickly through the whole forest. Her mind couldn't wrap around this. At all.

She must had been going insane. But everything looked so crude, so real.

She didn't like it.

The ashy, black trees were tall enough to reach the sky and the branches were thick enough to cover it, giving her a nauseating, frightening feeling. Everything was just so sickly dark, Arlette could feel things watching—lurking on her. She looked down at her feet, glancing at the hard ground that followed a path deep inside the forest. She looked hard at it—at its sickening cracks and its dull color. Arlette was going crazy. She must have. This couldn't be happening. Running her hand down her face, Arlette touched a dark, thorny bush nearby, her finger quickly feeling a stinging sensation.

Next thing she knew, droplets of red liquid oozed out of her and to the ground. "Blood," she whispered, astonished, knowing the smell more than anything else she knew.

Suddenly Arlette heard footsteps gain up on her, making her turn around sharply.

"Arlette." The frame before her said. It was Simone. Arlette looked at her, feeling overwhelmed by everything. She frowned, cocking her head and looking at Simone curiously. Simone was wearing a dark purple dress that screamed her name. Her bare arms were pale and filled with dark wisps embedded to her skin that began at her forearm and stopped at her knuckles. She was graceful but unnerving. Her plump lips were also a very dark purple...

"Why did you do this?" Arlette asked quietly, looking hard at her ode, dark eyes. Arlette didn't feel exactly happy at this...but then again, she didn't know what she was feeling lately.

Simone's purple lips found a smile, showing pearly white teeth. It was terrifying and beautiful at the same time, overwhelming and overpowering Arlette completely once again.

"I think you know the answer more than I do, my dear," she said smoothly, her high cheeks shining in the dimmed forest.

Immediately, a reminder crashed down on her like bricks.

Him.

Arlette backed away, her eyes locked with Simone's, realization dawning in her eyes.

Simone smiled again. A disturbing, enchanting smile. It reached her eyes, making them twinkle.

Arlette couldn't concentrate. As much as she tried, she couldn't try to communicate with him through her mind. She couldn't try to tell him that she was here. That she will always be here. Frustrated, Arlette shook her head, her gaze dropping from Simone's. She closed her eyes. "Please..." she whispered to herself. There has got to be more time, this couldn't be over—he couldn't be gone...he just couldn't.

Arlette turned around, with her eyes closed, and slowly, unsure, started to walk. Feeling her mind rattle and protest at the never stopping effort, she kept going, hearing Simone's voice behind her.

"You tried running away from a monster. But now you wish you were with him. Now you want to run to him," Simone laughed, her ominous, obnoxious laugh resonating through the whole forest. "I doubt you'll find him, dear, I really do. He is now only a memory..."

Arlette closed her eyes harder, screeching his name in her mind—trying to tell him that she was here, telling him to not let his fear consume him. But she got no response at all.

Her body ached and her soul tore apart at the realization, but she never stopped walking. She never stopped from silently praying to Fate to take her to him, to give him more time, to help her...

She really needed Fate's help. "Please..." Arlette silently begged as she walked faster, her eyes stinging with tears. "Take me to him. I am right here, his fear should be gone. It should be gone!" Arlette couldn't understand. She wasn't dead, she hadn't been taken away...hadn't she? This couldn't be happening. Why wasn't he responding? She wouldn't let the truth sink in - she wouldn't accept it.

Stubborn tears fell from her closed eyes, making her heart crack.

He's gone.

He's gone.

Arlette couldn't believe it. She kept walking stubbornly with her eyes closed, endless tears running down her face, her heart still telling her not to stop. But she had to. Nothing will bring him back now. Nothing.

Miserable sobs escaped her lips and she wished this wasn't true.

Simone was right. All along, everything Arlette tried to do was run away as far as she could from him. From the Beast. And now she was running to him, craving him, looking for him. Ironic, really. But what she was feeling before wasn't what she now felt. It will never be. She did tried everything she could to just ignore him and act like his existence wasn't enough to blow her mind. But it was. And she couldn't ignore the fact that she had willingly and reluctantly given her heart to him.

Suddenly, Arlette stopped abruptly, her sob stuck in her throat, no longer feeling the painful tug at her heart. But she felt the remaining ache, reminding her of how it felt to long for him.

Realizing that this was the end, that she needed to get out of here and find Daisy and go back to the palace, she painfully peeled her teary eyes open.

Only for her eyes to fall on a figure slumped against a tree.

She gasped.

Nobody had to tell her who it was.

She knew.

It was him.

It was Vince.

But how?

Regardless, Arlette found a weak smile through her tears.

But before she could do anything else and faster than she could process, Simone was in front of her, her eyes raging with something violent, disturbing, and frightening.

"How?" Simone hissed with a unhinged look upon her face. "How did you find him? You're not stronger than my powers—how?!" She pushed Arlette hard with abnormal force, making her shoot across the forest and slam against a tree.

Oppressive pain shoot through her back and all oxygen from her lungs was gone as she hit the raw tree and fell hard on the ground. But Simone didn't give her time to do anything, she was by her side in a second, yanking Arlette up on her feet and grasping her neck. Arlette was once again slammed against a tree, screams of pain and agony escaping her lips.

"Answer me!" Simone demanded, tightening her grip around Arlette's neck and lifting her off the ground.

"I...I don't know..." And she truly didn't. All she wanted to do was get away from Simone and go to him.

Her head was perilously spinning and her vision began to cloud with dark dots as she felt like she was losing herself. Her lungs ached terribly for oxygen as she felt even more suffocated by Simone's dead grip. Her nails dug and clawed into Simone's skin, trying to take her hands off of her neck desperately, the smell of Simone's blood filling her nose.

She was too powerful for Arlette.

Simone laughed maniacally. "You're such a liar. And for that, my sweetest Arlette, you will pay."

Before Arlette knew it, Simone's slender fingers accompanied by her whole hand were digging themselves into Arlette's chest, her other hand still around Arlette's neck. She felt intolerable pression as discomfort and pain shoot through her chest. Arlette screamed, fear smashing on her like rocks, feeling as Simone took hold of something inside of her. Something fragile. Something important.

Simone smiled. "Let's see how you'll live with your soul trapped in this forest."

Arlette waited to what seemed to be her end. Her thoughts went to him, her father, her sisters and everything she once held dear in her life. Even if she tried, she couldn't fight Simone. She held a savage, tormenting power that Arlette couldn't deal with. Tears streamed down her face as she weakly tried to fight her once again, all her remaining strength leaving her body.

"Don't even think about it, Simone."

Simone's head snapped towards the figure behind her.

"Mother? What are you doing here?" Simone sounded irritated but at the same time alarmed.

Arlette glanced at the woman with heavy eyelids threatening to shut her vision. The mysterious woman looked enthralling, like a goddess. Her presence itself was enough to let Arlette know that she held a great deal of power, even more than Simone's.

"Let her go, Simone. You have done more than enough." The woman's voice was smooth and calm, like Simone's when she was in the mood.

"You know I can't." Simone said as she snapped her head back toward Arlette, a hard expression on her face.

"You know what will happen if you do that. He's not dead yet." The woman said, walking towards Simone. "It will happen anyways, so just let her go. Let her go before I force you to."

But Simone made no move to free Arlette. Instead, she looked hard at her, hatred and maliciousness consuming the depths of her eyes. It was like she was having an internal battle with herself. But at the same time, it was like she had already made a decision.

"Even more reason to kill her. He needs to suffer like he made me suffer. He needs to see how easily she slithers from his grasp and how easily he loses her." Simone's voice was laced with coldness and without any remorse.

The woman sighed. "Simone, he found you with another man."

But Simone ignored her and made a move to snatch her hand out with whatever she had taken grasp of. Not before the woman took hold of Simone's shoulders, digging her black nails into her skin. "Let. Her. Go. Now."

Simone stopped, her eyes locked with her mother's. Arlette saw the resemblance. Same dark, big eyes, same plumped lips and body language. It was terrifying.

Slowly, her eyes still locked with her mother's, Simone let go of Arlette, taking her hand out of her chest and the other off of her neck.

Arlette breathed in sharply, kneeling on the ground as she struggled for breath. She coughed, her throat itching with pain.

Her chest stung and when she touched it there was nothing but her normal skin.

"Now," the mysterious woman began, "you no longer have the power that you're so used to have."

Arlette could see as Simone looked at her mother with furious eyes at this, but her mother continued. "You do not have power over him. Not anymore. Since she found him before the time had ended, you need to step back, Simone. You made him suffer enough. All these years—enough."

Simone shook her head feverishly, completely in denial. "You don't under-stand. He deserves this—"

"No, he doesn't." The woman said firmly, sighing. "I should've ended this the day you came home talking about throwing a deadly curse at the Prince. You have gone too far, Simone, way too far." The woman shook her head. "Now, go home and drink Lack. This is over."

Simone was flaming with rage as she glanced back at Arlette, saying. "We will see each other again." And before anyone knew it, Simone walked away from her mother, disappearing through thin air.

The mysterious woman was by Arlette's side in an instant, taking her arm and pulling her up on her feet. Arlette looked at her curiously, feeling weak, and the woman smiled warmly.

"It feels strange, doesn't it?" she asked, clarifying, "to see."

Arlette nodded, overwhelmed, her thoughts only on one thing.

The woman let go of her arm and smiled once again, moving out of her way. "Go."

Her eyes quickly fell on him.

He growled in pain, and slowly, dangerously, looked up at her direction. Her heart picked up erratically when his eyes met hers. But he was panting and was having difficulty trying to move, making Arlette worry to the point where she could no longer hold on and instead, go run to him and throw herself on the ground where he was. Tenderly, she put his head on her lap, holding each side of his face with her hands as tears mercilessly ran down her face. He was alarmingly hot, as if he had the fever. "Vince," she whispered, never looking away from his intense, dark gaze. "I thought you were gone…"

She looked down at him and at the blood oozing out of him in great chunks.

"Arlette." He said in a deep, exhausted voice, heavy emotion seething from it. It was the first time he said her name, which made her explode with a new set of thousands of different feelings. She slowly smiled and looked into his fathomless, dark eyes. He closed them, breathing deeply. "I thou ght…I thought you ran away." His voice dripped with an strong, unknown emotion that made Arlette's heart clench painfully and her stomach flutter with an overwhelming sensation.

She shook her head, never leaving his gaze. Delicately grazing his face with her fingertips, she stared at his perplexing, alluring scars and art. She couldn't deny the fact that actually seeing him was deliriously and frighteningly raw and baffling. But it didn't phase her. It didn't make a difference. She didn't feel frightened or grossed. She never had.

Arlette looked back at his eyes and she saw the realization in them. He hesitated before speaking. "…You can see me?"

Nodding, the tears never ceased to stop.

"...What do you see?"

She looked at his eyes, his nose, his lips, his hair, and all his unique, magnetic features. At his shoulders, his chest and all his body. "I...I see you. I see the monster and the man I know."

He looked at her with pain in his eyes. "You're not...?" He was referring to his face but Arlette shook her head. She wasn't petrified, or revolted. She couldn't bring herself to be.

Arlette looked up to see the woman standing nearby, eyeing her curiously.

"He's dying." Arlette uttered out to her, begging for her help.

The woman smiled slowly. "Well..." she drawled. "You know what to do."

Arlette slightly frowned but her lips found a small smile as well. She looked down at him and then at his ribs, where the blood was coming out in great portions. Slowly running her hand down his chest, she placed her hand on the huge wound, putting pressure on it. A low growl escaped from him.

She grimaced, whispering, "I'm sorry."

Closing her eyes, she concentrated. She didn't care if she was feeling weak, she desperately pulled and yanked for forces. Arlette could feel them hovering over her, teasing. And she ripped harder, breathing deep as they entered her body and thrashed viciously through her veins. They ran eagerly through her arms, exploding on her hands. She felt them ooze out of her and into the wound. It began to close.

Arlette knew that it would take him a few minutes to gain his strength back.

Retreating her hand, she peeled her eyes open, only to be met by his. They were two fascinating, fathomless depths of black seas. She felt like she could get lost in them. Smiling softly at him, involuntary tears streamed down her face. He placed his warm hand on her cheek and never stopped looking at her.

"Thank you." He said in a low voice, making her body melt.

She wanted to tell him that he didn't need to thank her, she would do it again if she had to with no hesitation. But no words left her lips.

"I think my time here has come to an end." The mysterious woman said, making Arlette look up at her direction. "I'm Gretta by the way. It was nice to know that neither of you would die today. Or ever...hopefully." She smiled mischievously, but it was playful, indicating that her words meant no harm.

Turning around, she started walking towards the dark trees, suddenly stopping and looking over her shoulder. "Oh, and you won't see Simone again. She thinks she can do whatever she wants, but she can't," Then she turned her head and started walking again.

"Wait!" Arlette called, making the woman stop and turn around.

Gretta rose a perfect sculpted eyebrow and looked at Arlette.

Arlette swallowed. "What...what about my sight?" She didn't know if it was supposed to go away or if she was going to stay like this. Either way, she wanted to know.

Gretta smiled. "It was a gift. Even if it was for bad intentions and ended up not working, it's still a gift. You cannot return gifts, so I'm afraid you'll have it for the rest of your days." She said softly, adding, "Besides, a soul as radiant as yours should not be cornered in darkness once again, eh?" The warm smile never left her lips as she winked at Arlette.

Arlette slowly returned the smile as Gretta turned around once again and was swallowed by the trees, not before she said, "The path will lead you to the exit. Farewell, my dear."

Moments after staring where Gretta disappeared, she felt his hand on her cheek once again, making her turn her face to his.

"My darling..." He said quietly as if not believing she was truly here with him. "I love you."

Arlette laughed quietly and took hold of his face with both of her hands once again. Those three words making her heart flutter and her soul cry. "My beautiful beast..." she kissed his lips, her next words having more meaning than they really do. "I love you more,"

Blind Beauty | 24 (Epilogue)

This wasn't meant to be this long but there were so many things that had to be covered so I was like why not? Okay, go read now.

EPILOGUE

Chapter Veinticuatro

Her grandmother, Lena—her mother, and sisters were in the living room, all stunned beyond belief at Arlette's gift. But, in all honesty, that was the least of her worries. She had to admit though, it was strange actually seeing her family, and their characteristics did impress her, but not for long.

Everything completely banished at the realization that she would never get to see her father's face.

She was back from the horrible forest. The Prince was in his room, resting. He had been taken there because he was very weak, something she hadn't expected. She thought he would regain his strength back right away, but he didn't, making the walk back outside the Dark Forest become brutal.

Daisy had been outside like she had promised, waiting as she sat under a tree at a fair distance away from the Dark Forest. It was dark, but night hadn't fallen entirely. When her tired eyes fell on Arlette, then the Prince, it was an understatement to say she was shocked and about to have a heart attack. Arlette had quickly explained to her and when Daisy nodded through her paranoia, she helped Arlette with the Prince. Now Daisy was somewhere in the palace, quickly skittering to the bathroom when the guardians helped them with the Prince, telling Arlette as she quickly walked away, "I've been holdin' it for so long, my poor bladder is gonna bust if I don't go now,"

The King, though. He was another story.

He was out still looking for his son, but Arlette sent word to him that he was here.

"How could you?"

Something frightening and vicious took over her eyes. "He was ruining everything! All these years, I've worked so hard...to have it all destroyed..." Lena shook her head madly. "I didn't want to do it. But he kept stopping me from doing my work when I was so close to—so close to—"

"To what? Killing me?" Arlette seethed, infuriated and shattered beyond belief. "How can you try to justify that? How can you try to justify your reason for killing father? There's no justification to that! You killed father, mom. You killed him!" Arlette glared ferociously at the figure a few feet away from her. She had brown, wavy hair that stopped just below her shoulders and brown eyes that glowed with something strange.

Her mother, who Arlette began to think she was not on her right mind.

She had never been, actually.

"Wait...what? Ember and Cade had both gasped in unison, their voices laced with utter horror and shock, making Arlette's head snap toward them. Both Ember and Cade looked at their mother; Cade staring at her with wide, crystal blue, frightened eyes and Ember on the verge of breaking down. Though Ember was the one who found her voice first, "...W-what you just said...Is that all...true? You can't be serious, mom, right? You didn't kill father. That's just crazy, right?"

Lena looked at Ember with an expressionless look upon her face, nodded once then said. "It's true,"

"Oh my God," Cade's voice was laced with terror, sorrow and disbelief. She covered her mouth with her hand and her eyes quickly welled up with tears, and she sobbed. Hard. Before Arlette could do anything, Ember was by Cade's side right away, pulling her close to her as she cried.

Arlette had never in her life encountered Cade break down like this, or even hear her cry. She'd always been a hard one to shed a tear, just like everyone else in her family, but Arlette understood.

Their mother had raised all three of them to not be soft. And unfortunately, Arlette sort of was. Her emotions were always known to the world and it was easy for her to let the tears fall freely. But at the same time, she could also hide her emotions and suppress her tears, it was just easier for her emotions to take over and control her.

"You can't be serious." Ember shook her head, looking at Lena with a bitter expression on her face as her voice rose and stubborn tears welled up her potent, green eyes. "I-I thought you said he wasn't 'bothering' you about that anymore! Out of all the things, mom! Really? You really had to do that? It was father for Lord's sake! Your husband, our dad, the...the best person on this sinful land!" Ember ran toward Lena, letting go of Cade, with a furious look upon her face as endless tears drowned her orbs, about to strike her, but Arlette came in the way, grabbing her and pulling her away at the last second.

Arlette stole a glance at her grandmother, and she wasn't surprised to see her unaffected at all of this, but for some reason, Arlette was eager to grab something and throw it at her for that.

Lena talked fast and Arlette began to think there was something seriously wrong with her. "Ember, you have to understand, I had to find out where that man really came from, where he was born, who conceived him, who made him the way he was, why Arlette is just like him. For all you know, she could be a threat—evil is everywhere—"

Evil. Arlette grew to loathe that word and all its concept now. "Evil...Ev il...Always thinking about evil being and coming everywhere! Evil has to be destroyed, we all know that." Arlette was so tired of everything, her own next words clenching and smashing her heart as she slowly let go of

Ember. "But you didn't have to kill him, mom. You didn't have to kill him. Father wasn't evil. He just believed I am not like that man. Now you're going to pay the consequences. But mom, I have a question...do I have to be destroyed according to you? Have I brought such great evilness and destruction upon your life that I have to be killed?"

Lena hesitated before speaking, seeming to try and pick out her words well, but Arlette held a hand up. "You know what? Don't even answer that. Let Fate forgive you for what you did." She mentioned a nod to the guardians who have been there all along. "Take her,"

After all, her mother didn't even try to apologize for her own sake, she was actually trying to justify what she did.

As Lena was taken by the guardians she yelped, her eyes wide, disbelief consuming them. "Arlette! What are you doing? Where am I being taken?"

"Some place far, far away." Arlette said as she shifted her gaze to her grand-mother.

Lena protested and screamed as the guardians took her away and Arlette looked away and closed her eyes, somehow making everything less harsh. Still, for some reason, her screams stabbed her soul. Arlette still loved her regardless. But what she did was a stronger, more painful reminder.

Arlette could hear her crying voice. "I'm your mother, Arlette! You can't do this to me! Please...forgive me!" She begged loudly, but nobody said anything or made a move. "Mother, do something!"

She opened her eyes and looked at her mother as she thrashed against the guardians' arms. Then at her grandmother.

"This only seems right, Lena." her grandmother said, regret covering her features, standing very still as she looked with an unknown expression at her daughter being taken away.

Another morbid scream made Arlette look up at her mother, who was being taken further away, nearing the big doors. "This is not over, Arlette! I had my reasons and I told you! I will always believe you're evil, because I know you are—"

The guardians finally dragged her out the door, shutting it tight behind them.

After that, there was a long, prickly silence.

Cade was shaking, Ember was intensely staring at the big doors and their grandmother had her eyes closed, collected.

And Arlette, she was just...there.

"I knew of this a long time ago." Her grandmother began, cutting the heavy silence, and opening her wrinkly, grey eyes. "I didn't say anything because Lena had threatened me to do the same to me if I ever did I say a word." She paused, sighing. "Forgive me,"

Arlette glanced at her grandmother at this, not sure if to believe her or not. So many things have happened that have completely tattered and ripped her ability to believe and trust...now it was almost impossible for her to believe her grandmother.

So she couldn't help herself but say, "For forgiveness, you could always pray, grandma."

"Arlette," said Ember quietly, not letting her grandma respond, walking toward Arlette and embracing her in a warm hug, her voice heavy with emotion, "I'm truly sorry for the way I treated you. Mom is very sick in the head. She wanted to make me sick too, and I almost let her." She paused, her voice covered with pain and regret. "You don't have to forgive me now, just know that you're honestly the best sister I could possibly have. I should've never treated you the way I did."

Ember pulled away and Arlette stared at her. At her long, blond hair, her high, pink cheekbones, her green orbs, and all her features. She was taller than Arlette, and truly beautiful. Arlette wanted to touch her face.

"Arlette," It was another voice.

A familiar male's voice.

Her head snapped towards him.

"Aaron." Arlette said flatly but sort of glad.

He had come from another door from the same living room, looking quite stressed from what Arlette could gather by the way he walked toward her and by the way his muscles tensed. And that was when she let her eyes take him in.

Aaron had striking blond hair that stopped at his shoulder blades and honey-colored eyes that gave away too much about him. He had a firm jaw line and thick eyebrows. A incredibly strong body, and veins running beneath the skin of his hands, showing just how strong he was.

It still fascinated her how everyone was just uniquely and terrifyingly beautiful in their own way.

It seemed as if Aaron was in a hurry.

He embraced her unexpectedly, not affecting Arlette as he quickly tried to apologize. "I'm so sorry, Arlette. I was under a spell last night. I didn't—"

"I know," Arlette mumbled against his chest. "It's okay," she said as she pulled away and looked at him.

Maybe it wasn't normal to just look at people. But Arlette wasn't exactly used to it, so she willingly swallowed every feature she saw in someone, reluctantly fascinating her. Along with all their facial expressions and how they gave away too much about people and their feelings.

Or maybe it was just easier for her to read people.

"I heard of what happened. Are you okay?" Concern covered his features and Arlette nodded, not really sure if she was indeed okay.

"Good," he said, nodding, seeming satisfied. "I'd stay but I've got to go. My father hasn't come back and that's not very usual of him."

Arlette nodded and looked to see his hand run through his long hair.

A wave of worry came over her. She had already sent word to the King that he needed to come back. Why wasn't he back? It had been a while now.

Arlette tried not to worry too much.

But didn't work very well.

Kissing Arlette on the cheek, Aaron said his farewells, and in his way, Ember was briefly blocking him. She moved to let him pass, but when she did, so did he. They were both trying to let each other pass, which caused them both to be in each other's way. Ember smiled, the awkward situation pushing her to the verge of bursting out in laughter despite the tension in the room. Things like these always made Ember laugh. Aaron smiled too. And they smiled at each other, looking at one another like they'd never seen each other until now, and it was like they were having a silent conversation. But finally, Ember slid to right, letting him pass.

Arlette could see as her sister's cheeks reddened very briefly.

Aaron walked passed Ember slowly and to the big doors, opening them and shutting them behind him, not before giving Ember a last glance.

"Where is Lena being taken?" Her grandmother asked suddenly.

Arlette glanced at her. "To her second cousin. Heather."

Heather was a specialist in dealing with people like her mother. And she lived all the way on the other side of the Fae Lands.

Her grandmother nodded, understanding but looking as if she was getting sick. "You'll have to excuse me. I need to rest,"

Arlette nodded and her grandmother left the room.

There was a moment of silence.

"We're not going to seem mom ever again…are we?"

Arlette shook her head gingerly, looking at her sister, Cade. "Most likely. She needs to spend some time with Heather."

"You do know mom hates her endlessly, right?" Cade raised an eyebrow. There was a light smile gracing her lips, which brightened the gloomy atmosphere around them. Cade really knew just how hilarious and ridiculous was Lena's hate for Heather.

For Lena, staying with her cousin would be her worst nightmare.

"Yes. But Heather's patience is like steel. Remember that time when we kept poking her with a stick for thirty minutes straight?" Arlette recalled, briefly smiling at the memory. "She didn't even seem bothered."

"I do. Lords! I could not stop laughing. It's ridiculous how much patience she has. Remember that time when grandma was on her way from Benny's and Heather was waiting for her, standing outside for almost two hours without a single complaint? Just too much." Cade shook her head, smiling as well.

"I can already see mom's face when she knows where she's being taken," Ember added. She was sitting in one of the luxurious sofas nearby. "I remember when we were out with both of them and mom was just desperate for that healer to finish preparing the herbs while Heather just kept on making endless conversations with him,"

"Me too," inquired Cade, nodding. "Heather is amazing, I don't understand how mom could possibly hate her,"

Arlette shrugged, following Cade as she sat on one of the sofas and Arlette sat on another one. The living room was enormous, with a shiny, impeccable marble floor, tall windows with beautiful curtains, and stunning furniture. "Mom doesn't like a lot of people,"

Both Cade and Ember nodded, agreeing, Cade saying, "True,"

"I think I like Lord Aaron," Ember suddenly blurted out after a long moment of silence.

"Who don't you like?" Cade inquired, her eyes rolling.

Arlette smiled. It was true. Ember liked anybody, really. But she could see how Aaron had suddenly taken a soft spot in her reckless heart.

"No, I'm serious," she said. "I don't know...it was weird but the way he looked at me..." Ember shook her head. "Lords, I sound like a little girl with sappy feelings,"

"And you hate feelings," Arlette finished, smiling despite everything.

"Exactly."

"Well," started Cade as she put one leg over the other, "hopefully you won't break his heart."

Ember glared at Cade, shooting invisible daggers at her. "I don't break hearts," she confessed, pausing, but then softening her gaze. "Well...not that many."

Arlette gasped. "Ember!"

Ember burst out laughing, flipping her hair. "Not my fault I can't seem to fall for a man,"

☐

Arlette went up the endlessly tiring stairs, eagerness spreading throughout her veins.

She ran the endless halls, almost stumbling with her own feet.

She didn't know how she recognized, after a few turns, that this was the right door out of the many doors in the halls, but it was sort of obvious.

It was the largest and biggest door and it stood out like a morbid scream within the calm. It had eccentric designs and foreign shapes.

Arlette grabbed one of the golden, shiny handles, clicking it open, and quietly pulling the door open.

It overwhelmed her how big the room was—just like everything else. Even in the dark, she could see that it was decorated with gripping paintings and long heavy curtains. As she closed the door behind her, she could see a crystal balcony door at the other end of the room, where the moon shone high and bright, illuminating through the crystal and inside the room. Her eyes fell on the humongous, luxurious four post bed where he was. But he was too far away from the light, where she could barely make him out.

Arlette was so eager to see him and she didn't even know why.

She quietly walked over to the other side of the bed, feeling nervous as she just stood there, seeing her own shadow reflect in front of her, debating whether or not to get in the bed with him. Maybe she was getting a little ahead of herself. He was exhausted and needed to rest.

Arlette shook her head to herself, turning around to go back outside and let him rest. How could she just—

"Where are you going?"

His deep, compelling voice reached her ears, freezing her in spot for a second, before she gingerly turned around. "I...I thought..." Arlette couldn't make out the words, so she just sighed and slowly, carefully got into bed with him.

When her body landed on the bed, he quickly pulled her close to him, wrapping a strong, bare arm around her waist.

He was indeed strong, far more stronger than Aaron--and Aaron was very strong. She felt like he could break her—or anything, really—in half with the slightest, most insignificant effort.

Without thinking, she placed her head on his bare chest and his muscles seemed to ripple as he put his arm around her.

She smiled to herself when she heard the strong steady beat of his heart, her fingers grazing over his torso, touching the familiar wisps. "How are you feeling?" Arlette asked softly as she picked up her head and looked at him. She could barely make out his features in the dark, which she wasn't very fond of. But his scent and voice were enough to push her over the edge.

"Better," he said, his voice low and Arlette could feel as his chest rumbled when he said that.

Her lips slowly quirked up into a smile and she nodded, relief washing over her. She had been worried about him all this time since he'd been taken by the guardians and healers, wondering if there was something bad enough to make her worry even more than she already was.

Arlette couldn't help but to shift in place in a comfortable position to let herself touch him.

Her fingertips tenderly ran from the bottom of his torso, and his body tensed, to his collarbones, his neck, and he growled, and to his face. Then his hair. It was thick and long, dark, loose curls softly curling around her fingers.

"You're killing me," he growled as he breathed deeply, suddenly grabbing her wrist and stopping her.

Arlette gasped, realizing how naive she had been to—

"I...I'm...so—"

He brought her hand down to his lips and kissed her knuckles, making Arlette want to explode and disappear all at once. Something jolted inside of her and her whole body began to tug and ache as whispers teased her ears.

She closed her eyes, enthralled by the feel he gave her.

And before she knew it, she was fired beneath his warm body just like last time. His touch made Arlette's blood burn in a way that burst up to her skin and once again, made her want to explode and shatter into a million pieces beneath him.

Low, menacing growls escaped his lips as he placed them on her neck, his touch seeming to both corrupt her and make her burst out pure and alive,

"I'm trying to control myself. I do not want to hurt you. My darling, you're so fragile—"

"I'll be fine," Arlette whispered, pausing, and reassuring him with a small smile as she took his face in her hands.

This close, she could see his coal-black, captivating eyes. They were so entrancing, so intense. She felt like he could see through her eyes and into her soul.

And at that moment Arlette knew that it'd be fine. That everything will. Arlette, no mattered the many times she had tried to deny it, loved him with every fiber of her being; she loved all of him, like she had never loved anyone else. It burned. It burned like rum on a fire the way she had grown to feel such intensity towards him; such affection, such love so pure and overpowering she wanted for him to hold her close forever and kiss her and never let go.

Because she knew, deep down, this will last forever.

He loved her. Intensely, deadly, powerfully. He loved her in a way that could've made any woman envious of just the way he thought of her. He'd always looked at her like she was the only piece of art in the world, like her whole being was air and he couldn't breathe. She was different. Fascinating. Pure. Vince was filled with coldness, darkness, and emptiness. But she'd melted all of that with the flames that burst out of her like impatient volcanoes and splashed on him feverishly. And in all honesty, he would never get enough of her. Never. She will always be his beauty. His Princess. His love. The one who had ripped and taken his heart from his chest. The only one he gave permission to do that and always will.

□　　□　　□　　□　　□　　□　　□

SIX MONTHS LATER.

Ember's P.O.V.

"Ember! Goodness, can you stop? I'm actually scared for my life right now."

"I'm telling you, Daisy, I know how to cook! I swear it. Now, calm down and come back here."

A frightened expression took over Daisy's features as her eyes stayed glued on the sharp object in the crazy, wavering hands of Ember. "Not with that knife you have in your hand! You almost chopped off my poor peetee sticky,"

"Your poor what?" Ember frowned, narrowing her eyes as she tried to decipher one of the many strange words Daisy usually used.

"My finger, woman! You almost chopped it off!"

Ember rolled her eyes as she took a handful of leaves and threw them in the pot. "Oh, come on, Daisy. You're being dramatic. You moved it just before I could actually cut it."

Daisy's eyes were wide as she slowly started to walk back near Ember. "Exactly! And we're not even cooking. We're makin' tea, Ember. Tea."

Ember huffed. "Isn't that still considered making something? As in cooking?"

"Well...not exactly," Daisy answered warily. "We're just choppin' long herbs and—"

"Yes it is. I told you, I know how to cook. Not that much though..." Ember confessed slowly. "That's why I need your help!" Her hands began wavering again like crazy as she exclaimed and Daisy yelped, going down just before the knife could reach her face.

"Lords! You know what? I can't do this anymore—today is not my day to die. I give up. Bye." Daisy turned around sharply and stormed off.

"Daisy!" Ember called, laughter stumbling out of her lips. "I'm sorry!" She could hear Daisy huff and stomp her feet like a five year old. When Ember didn't get a response and Daisy kept walking, she called again, "Come back when you feel ready to die!" And Ember couldn't help herself but keep laughing guiltily at Daisy's paranoia.

Right after Daisy exited the kitchen, Arlette came in, frowning as she saw Ember grabbing onto her sides.

"What's so funny?" Arlette asked, smiling at her sister.

Ember shook her head. "I swear Daisy will still have to help me learn how to cook." She looked at Arlette, grinning, secretly thinking about getting revenge on Daisy for leaving her alone to finish making the tea.

Arlette chuckled. "I told you she truly does get scared by anything,"

Ember shook her head again, fixing her hair as she pushed the strands away from her face. "Well, she has got to learn how to live a little, and I'm going to teach her just that,"

Arlette shook her head too at Ember, knowing how reckless Ember can be. "What you need to do is tell me why Aaron is so furious. He has given everybody a cold shoulder for the past few days. What did you do to him this time?"

It was true. Aaron had been and was beyond furious. And with Ember he always was. They always argued like a married couple when they weren't even remotely close to being in a relationship.

But then again, it was sort of complicated.

"Me? I didn't do anything!" Ember said defensively. "That's his own problem. He keeps telling me not to go out so much." Ember rolled her eyes. "We're not even together. We've never been—so I don't understand why he's trying to be protective. Like no. I can clearly take care of myself, I don't need a man to play guardian for me. I've been doing that just fine,"

Both of Arlette's eyebrows rose and she smiled warmly at her sister. "He cares for you, you know that, right? You two are just too stubborn to admit the fact that you'd both die for each other,"

As much as Ember wanted to deny it, it was true. Tragically so. But it scared her—the intense feelings she had towards him; feelings she had never felt for any man before.

And she didn't like it.

So she denied it regardless. "Woah, Arlette, wait up a minute. It's kind of obvious the hatred we have for each other...I wouldn't exactly die for him..."

"But isn't there a thin line between love and hate?"

"There is," Ember answered, her stomach sinking for no coherent reason.

Arlette sighed, tucking a strand of red, fiery hair behind her ear as she changed the subject. "Mom is coming to visit us today."

Ember frowned at this. "She is?"

Arlette nodded.

Ember smiled at Arlette, her sister's hazel eyes reminding Ember of her father's. "It's going to be okay. Remember what I told you?"

Arlette nodded once again, a smile slowly reaching her lips.

They both remembered.

Arlette was one of most powerful beings in the whole entire Lands. She had learned to toy with her many abilities and with abstract forces. With endless effort and constant patience, she had learned to master them all. She was as powerful as someone could be. And she could control it all it. She wasn't destructive or evil. She was power. Gifted. And Ember had herself learned how to improve her abilities as well in the mists of helping Arlette with hers.

They had, all three of them, slowly coped with their father's death. Not entirely, though, but they were getting there. Very slowly.

Arlette was also coping with the fact that she was given sight. Ember knew it was still overwhelming and terrifying for her. This world was too raw and crude to look at, but she was doing relatively amazing. And she no longer hid under her mother's—or anyone's—cloak anymore. Arlette had become independent and strong willed. She was not longer the naive, shy girl that Ember grew to know. She was far more than that.

And finally, after so much chaos, everything was getting fine, or seeming to be. Almost perfect even.

But none of this was over.

It will never be.